theLast Resort

the Last Resort

Scenes from a Transient Hotel

By Aggie Max

CHRONICLE BOOKS

SAN FRANCISCO

For Diana, Sheila, and Jan Wall who taught me how.

Printed in the United States of America.

Library of Congress Cataloging-in-Publication Data:
Max, Aggie.
    The last resort : scenes from a transient hotel / by Aggie Max.
    176 p.   15.3 x 23 cm.
    ISBN 0-8118-1285-5 (hc)
    1. Poor women — California — Oakland — Biography. 2. Homeless women —
    California — Oakland — Biography. 3. Single-room occupancy hotels —
    California — Oakland. I. Title.
    HV4046.02M39   1997
    362.83'092 — dc21   96-47136
    [B]   CIP

Book and cover design: Laura Lovett
Composition: On Line Type
Cover: *The Scream* by Lillian Bassman © 1994. Silkscreen-photograph.

Distributed in Canada by Raincoast Books
8680 Cambie Street
Vancouver BC V6P 6M9

10 9 8 7 6 5 4 3 2 1

Chronicle Books
85 Second Street
San Francisco, CA 94105

Web Site: www.chronbooks.com

Contents

1. The Rules

There are few people who would want to visit me in my present state. Maybe no one.

This is why the sign in the lobby, NO VISITORS AFTER FIVE P.M., has a delayed impact on me. It hangs prominent amidst an array of other signs announcing various other rules, rules about keys, towels, noise, food, etc.

This is not the Hyatt Regency after all, I think. It is a transient hotel in downtown Oakland. I lived in plenty of transient hotels in the 1960s. I just don't remember NO VISITORS and all these other rules posted behind the desk. Maybe They should print up a little pamphlet like they give you in the city jail. Then they could put up a nice painting on the wall behind the desk. Or a *mirror....*

There is a saying which my friend Adeline likes to repeat: "It's a sorry rat that only has one hole." I guess this one is going to be mine.

I have an impulse toward hysterical laughter. I control it. Then I think: What if someone came to visit me, and they couldn't get in? Not likely, but What *if?* I am holding my wrists out for the handcuffs, sticking my neck in the noose. What happens if somebody comes to visit me and it's after five o'clock?

A voice says in my head: "We don't let them in. We don't let them go up. We let this, but not that. We let, we don't let. We make the rules."

"Who are you to fucking *let* me do anything?" I want to scream. "Who are you to let anybody do one thing and not do something else? Who *are* you?"

"We are the owners. We own the place. You own nothing. Simple as that. We make the rules. You read the signs, follow the rules, pay rent, or we kick you out in the street. See how lucky you are to have a nice room, clean sheet and towel. Lucky you."

Dudley, my roommate-to-be, must have sensed me stiffening up in front of the desk. "Come see the room, Ash," he says brightly, gripping my elbow with some force. "It's nice. You'll like it."

Dudley wouldn't have to worry about visitors. Who would visit *him?*

A few days later my daughter Jessy stops by the hotel after work. She's bringing some laundry I'd asked her to wash for me.

"Sorry," says the guy at the desk, a parolee who lives in terror of the owners' power to take away his job.

"What?" Jessy recoils in disbelief. "I can't go up and see my *Mom??*"

"Sorry. Against the rules."

"What is this, *prison?*"

"Rules," mumbles the Desk Guy.

Jessy shoves the laundry onto the desk, trying to stuff it into the slot beneath the bars behind which the Desk Guy works. "Then *you* take this up to my mom. It's her laundry. She needs it."

The Desk Guy shrugs. "Sorry. I can't leave the desk." He is beginning to feel uneasy, unable to look at this woman whom he is telling she can't visit her own mother, in a hotel room for which Mom pays upwards of $100 a week, because it's after five P.M.

"OK," he finally says. "You go on up. But just for a minute. It's my job."

Somebody bangs on the door. Dudley almost falls off his chair. I close the book I'm reading, marking the place with my finger. I am more startled than scared.

The banging continues. Dudley is looking at me hopefully, as though I would know what to do better than he. "Should I open it?" he whispers.

"Open up, it's me!" comes a muffled voice from the hall outside.

"Open it," I shrug.

Dudley opens the door and there is Jessy, in a mild rage. She tosses the laundry bag into the room.

"It's Jessy," says Dudley.

"Here's your shit," says Jessy. "I gotta go." She disappears down the hall toward the stairs.

"How rude," I sigh. I've disappointed the Children again.

"It was only Jessy," says Dudley.

"Strike one for Family Values."

Journal Entry: The endless heaping of small irritations and disappointments; by this you know you're still alive. No sense of victory or overcoming, no progress made, just a taste of sour unfairness. The little pleasures too heavily outnumbered—you can't trust them. . . .

Not enough energy to sustain a rage or a creative effort. Available energy is used trying to recover from the impact and shock of countless petty blows, none worth fighting about or even trying to protect oneself from. An attitude usually somewhere between indifference and dull anger. Life at this point is mainly an unpleasant sensation. The body and its needs an annoyance. I've always been somewhat out of synch with the rest of society, but rarely so out of synch with myself. I have so little perspective. Self-analysis is like trying to pick up the rug you're standing on.

How much more bearable if the Children didn't see me living like this. "My mom, the Bag Lady." Jessy will laugh it off. Still, she'll want to call and talk. If I had a phone. Can't believe there aren't even any phone jacks in these rooms. Pay phone in the lobby, usually broken. Twenty-one years old and only six months out of the nest, Jessy will resent being cut off from Mom like this. I should file a complaint. But who would listen?

Anyway, Family Values having more or less struck out, we now get Friendship to the plate.

Adeline, my best and only friend, shows up a week later, panting and sweating profusely. Dudley opens the door. Adeline staggers into the room and falls onto the bed.

"Those *stairs!*" She gasps.

"You get used to them." I apologize.

"*You* get used to them." She is in a fermenting state, trying to decide whether she should be pissed off, glad to see me, or just exhausted.

"This guy downstairs at the desk ..." she begins, looking guilty.

"Oh god. What did you do to poor Terence?"

"I didn't do nothing to the motherfucker. It's what he did to *me.* He said I couldn't come up!"

I look at Dudley's $2.98 alarm clock. "It's only three o'clock."

"He said I had to give him my I.D. before I could come up."

"You give them your I.D.," I explain. "They put it in the mailbox for the room. When you leave, you go to the desk and they give it back."

Adeline is listening patiently. "Yeah, that's what he said." She removes a plastic mineral-water bottle from her huge shoulder bag. Dregs are sloshing around in the bottom of the bottle. She chugs down the dregs. The room fills with the aroma of vodka. "But I don't *have* any I.D. I mean, I don't drive, so I don't have a drivers' license. And I went to apply for an I.D. card but it didn't come yet. I had to stand on line four hours at the DMV to get my picture took for *that* motherfucker! And I got my Medi-Cal card but it's last month's and it don't have my picture on it. Thank god."

"So you had a horrible fight with the Desk Guy." I close my eyes to get a better picture of the scene in my head.

"I had to give him my *keys*. It was all I had. So he takes my keys and puts them in a box and says I can come on up. I shoulda known better. Those stairs! How are you, my dear?"

"It's lovely to see you, my dear. Do you have any money?"

And she has some money, so we send Dudley out for a gallon of wine to celebrate the Good Old Days, and later we send him back out for a bag of Nathon's Huge Hamburgers, and by that time we are all pretty well done for.

It gets dark, maybe eight or nine P.M., and the guy at the desk still hasn't summoned the courage to come up and evict Adeline from my room. But she's ready to leave. So I say, foolishly but according to custom, "I'll walk you to the bus stop, my dear."

We stagger down the hall and I get her down the stairs somehow without damage, and she steadies herself and walks to the desk. The Desk Guy cringes when he sees her coming. Adeline has that effect on people. She stomps to the desk and says in a huge, booming, very Black voice "My keys!!"

The guy spins around and reaches into the mailbox for Room 407 and spins back around to hand Adeline a monstrous ball of keys weighing maybe two pounds.

"*Thank* you, sir," says Adeline, with a totally poisonous look.

"Madam!" exclaims the Desk Guy.

"Cool it," I tell Adeline in a loud whisper, "This guy is on parole for murder. He's dangerous. He just got out of San Quentin."

She gives me an extra long look, as if to say "*Must* you tell me things like this?"

Friendship scores.

Journal Entry: Sledgehammer emotions, but a sledgehammer wrapped in layers and layers of cotton. Not the sharp, pointed, needling little pokes which you can focus on because they never let up—just *boom!* get it right out, and you're left to deal with it however you can if you can.

You don't know what you've been hit with, or even that you've been hit, for weeks, months, years. No open, bleeding wounds. Just perturbations, endless perturbations of the spirit, pulling you in all different directions. Maybe They think it evens itself out after a while, and that if you get hit from one side this week and the other side next week it will seem as if you haven't been hit at all and you can manage to stay straight. It doesn't work that way. You just get weaker and weaker and never know why, or how to fight back. They set you spinning, and you're pretty much lost, blindfolded, pushed this way and that by invisible hands.

2. The Hotel

Trudging up the stairs in the hotel I pass a woman who is trudging down. Young, maybe late twenties, with the look of an old Basset hound — resigned, cowed, begging for mercy, a drooping blob of a woman, even the eyeballs seem to be drooping out of their sockets in defeat.

She is descending the stairs as a child would, with both feet on one step before attempting the next, putting all her effort into getting down the darned stairs.

I can hear the little voice in the woman's head patiently instructing: "OK. Now step down one step. *There* you go. OK. Now bring the other foot down next to the first foot. Good! Now let go of the handrail and move the hand down about fourteen inches. OK. Now step down to the next step with your right foot. Good. Now the left. . . ."

A flabby little blob woman. The eyes, the mouth, the whole face seem to be sliding off the sides of the skull and down, as though gravity were trying to make a joke or a visible statement with this person totally out of synch and in a losing battle with gravity.

I risk a tiny bit of eye contact, enough to see that there is nothing much in those eyes which look out of some kind of abysmal pit of hopelessness. The woman catches me looking and responds with an I've-forgotten-how-to smile. One corner of the droopy mouth twitches up a quarter of an inch for half a second. The eyes don't change.

"Sorry," says the woman. This statement can be interpreted in so many different ways that it is impossible to respond to. This is one person to whom you cannot say "Have a nice day." Ever.

As I struggle up to the step where the blob-woman is standing (hearing the voice say "The foot first, then the hand. Move the foot *before* you move the hand. You don't have to let go of the railing, OK? just slide the hand down . . . and now the other foot. . . .")

The woman offers another little tic of a smile, then says "I hafta go get somethin' to eat. 'Cause I'm pregnant." And continues on down the stairs, one step at a time.

A few days later, struggling up the stairs, I find the droopy woman sitting in the stairwell between the second and third floors of the hotel. "I got this awful cold and I dunno what to do," the woman explains. "And I keep sneezing alla time, and my nose keeps running, and what should I *do?*" The woman is almost crying. "What should I *do??*"

"It will go away," I say, continuing up the stairs. The woman does not seem reassured.

Journal Entry: In a situation like this, one really gets a chance to see the laws of gravity, entropy, momentum and inertia at work. Everything is in the process of slowing down, breaking or being broken down, including people. Even the pay phone in the lobby is "out of order." That's four flights of stairs and one and a half blocks to the nearest working phone, eight flights and three blocks round-trip to make a phone call. Everything that moves, including water and electricity, has to be suspect. Everything that moves can just as easily stop moving, and probably will, unexpectedly and just when you need it most. People are affected by all this, as people are affected by all nature's laws, whether they realize it or not. We spend most of our time and energy struggling with things which most people in this country take for granted.

The building is old and well built, of smooth beige bricks with orna-mental cornices and ledges. At one time it must have been a good hotel. The lobby is large, with a fourteen-foot ceiling and mirrored from waist-height to moldings, although many of the mirror panels are missing.

Entering through the glass double doors from the street and walking toward the stairs, one passes on the left a row of vending ma-chines for soft drinks and candy, and a pay phone in a wooden booth. To the right a console TV is the focus of a couple of floral-patterned sofas and chairs, which look comfortable enough but creak of card-board when one sits down. The TV is set against the plate glass win-dows, which run the length of the front of the lobby. Alone on the knee-high window ledge, halfway between the TV and the glass doors, sits a cactus in a small pot.

At the back of the lobby to the right of the stairs is a long wooden counter behind which the Desk Guy sits. A heavy metal security fence runs from the top of the counter to the ceiling. On the wall behind the counter is a bank of wooden cubicles for mail and keys, along with the signs explaining rules and regulations. The rest of the ground floor, which might once have held the hotel's bar, restaurant and kitchen, has been partitioned off and rented to other sleazy businesses which I sus-pect are mainly fronts for even sleazier businesses.

The stairs begin at the right of the elevator, continue around be-hind, and emerge on the other side of the elevator shaft on the next floor. The elevator has never been converted to self-service, so that when it is used, which is seldom, the Desk Guy must emerge from be-hind the desk, lock up his cage, and operate the thing manually. It is small, creaky, scary, and very very slow.

The building is seven stories high, shaped like a capital E, with the main hallways running through its spine. There are two rooms in each arm of the E and ten opening off the main corridor, sixteen rooms per floor above the lobby. On each floor, on either side of the central stairway are small rooms containing a bathtub, a garbage can, a metal shower stall, a locked mystery closet, and two rooms with toilets.

Journal Entry: Tuesday is supposed to be the day for "maid service" in the hotel, but the cart didn't show up today. They usually come around between one and two P.M., banging on the doors, and you can exchange your dirty sheets and towels for clean ones if you want them. The linen comes in two shades of off-white—grey/white and yellow/white—with the names of various hospitals printed on it. The toilet in the hall hasn't been cleaned in two weeks, and the lightbulb is gone again. The "maids" are two young Indian guys who apparently don't speak English. The elevator is still out of order.

I don't wish to complain, just to describe. Complaining doesn't help anyway. People will just tell you you're lucky to have any place to stay at all. Still, it seems that $480 a month is a lot to pay for one mosquito-infested room with four flights of stairs to climb and a filthy toilet in the hall. There must be some set of rules somewhere governing the operation of these places. They have rules for every other goddamned thing, don't They?

Journal Entry: I don't want to live in this place. It's dirty, depressing, dangerous, and much too expensive. It stinks of despair and desperation. It's a lesson in demoralization.

> But you *are* desperate. You are lucky to be able to afford this place. The room is actually not so bad, as rooms go: it has a door that locks, a window that can be opened, running water. Actually, you're *lucky* to have this room.

But it's a trap.

> Anywhere can be a trap.

I have no money.

> Money is a trap.

I can't go anywhere.

Where do you want to go?

I don't know.

Also, I have to share it with this guy. I don't want to share it with anyone. I want my own room.

Here's a guy I sat down next to on the bus once because all the other seats were taken, and now what if I have to live with him in this room forever?

Aren't you lucky to have this person to live with? Aren't you lucky to have somebody?

He would rather live alone, too. Have his own room. But neither of us can afford it.

So I guess I'm lucky to have someone to share the rent. The rent, the rent. One must pay the rent, the rent, the rent, the rent.

3.

Dudley

It is often hard for me to talk myself into getting out of bed. "Get out of *bed!*" I scream at myself, silently. "But bed is *safe*," I explain to the screamer. "At least *so* far."

I tell myself that I can begin anew; I am no longer the same person I was when I had my own apartment and made my own rules. "Whatever it was that You thought you were doing," I tell that person, "It didn't work. Or *I* wouldn't be *here*." "Oh, right!" My former self sneers. "Easy for you to blame everything on Me!"

"The Navy has this ship," Dudley says. He is talking to me. He must want something. "It's totally manned by women."

"I'm not getting out of bed," I inform him.

"We call it the Love Boat, in the yard." Dudley works in a shipyard when he's not laid off. "It's a supply ship and machine shop. Most of the chicks are welders and machinists. They're mostly dogs, but they got some nice looking ladies too."

"They could fix their own ship, instead of making *you* do it."

"Of course, most of them are bulldykes," Dudley goes on. "They come in this bar where we go after work. They tear it up."

"You lie."

"Well, maybe," he admits. "Are you gonna buy me a six-pack or not?"

I rummage through the pile of stuff on the floor on my side of the bed. "Manned by women. I love it." I give Dudley a ten. "Get me some wine, the usual. And ice."

"You have a bad attitude, Ash," says Dudley, his usual complaint. Focused totally on his six-pack of beer he forgets ice, and the chablis is warm, so I send him back out.

"My totem is the slug," I say, pointing to the door.

"What?" He doesn't understand. He doesn't understand much.

"I thrive on toxic sludge. I like it cold."

He closes the door behind him on his way out, very quietly.

Dudley likes to sit in the room's only chair, an armless torture rack of fake gilt tubing with a green plastic seat. He will not get into bed until whenever he has decided is his official bedtime, at which point he takes off all his clothes and puts on his old-man pajamas.

"My wife bought me these pajamas for my birthday, when I was married," he says every time he puts them on, part of the ritual of official bedtime. All I know about his ex-wife is that she is a Brooklyn Jew. Dudley must have been her rebellion against fate; she probably thought he was the perfect Goy, blond blue-eyed middle class middle American farm boy from the midwest sort of myth. They worked, made money, bought a house with a pool, drove nice cars, had no kids. She probably bought the pajamas as a joke. Old-man cotton pajamas with buttons and elastic, innocuous vertical blue stripes, made for a nursing-home patient. Woke up the next morning and there he was sleeping next to her, actually *wearing* them. "She wanted to have kids and I didn't," Dudley tells me. "My family is mentally disturbed anyway. If I had kids, they'd all be fucked up in the head. Besides, I didn't want any. So we got a divorce."

She got the house with the pool, the furniture, the TV, and

the stereo. He got to keep his car and these pajamas. The car got repossessed.

Someone is screaming in the street. The screams echo down the corridors of the street, bouncing off brick and glass, amplified into surreal horror. Nobody calls the police, and the screams eventually die down of their own accord. I finish my last glass of cold wine and lie down to sleep, trying to find comfort in the cracks on the ceiling.

When he's not watching his little black-and-white TV, Dudley reads. He reads only non-fiction because his thought-processing apparatus is not sufficiently developed to understand fiction, or even the concept of fiction. He reads heavy books about science and advanced mathematical calculations related to physics. Does he understand this stuff? I don't understand a word of it, so how can I say that he *doesn't* assimilate it in some idiot-savant fashion?

I've learned by sneaking in sly questions that Dudley believes reading to be the equivalent of understanding. "I read it, therefore I understand it." The act of reading itself may be a magical and mystical act for him, perhaps a kind of meditation. Or it may just be what he does to keep the little wheels in his head from rusting.

It would have been nice if the god of propinquity had sat me down next to somebody I could talk to, but how often does that happen?

Journal Entry: You can no longer move forward. Your natural movement into the future is interfered with, or maybe you've just run out of fuel.

You find yourself just going round and round, sometimes faster, sometimes slower, but always in the same meaningless circles.

The hotel is full of people going round in mean little circles. Couldn't all this energy be used for something better, somehow?

It's lonely at the bottom.

· · ·

"When I was growing up," I say to Dudley, or in the direction of Dudley's abstracted form, "I was a pariah. Do you know what that is?"

He rolls his eyes toward me. I can hear him thinking: You and your fancy words. Sometimes I think you make them up, to fuck with my head. "No," he says. "I give up."

"An outcast, a reject from society. It was because of my family, who were very poor and on welfare, and they were Communists to boot. Everything was political."

"I hate politics," says Dudley.

"So I was like shit on the sidewalk, with everybody avoiding me and watching where they stepped. That was me, growing up. Only you never do grow up."

Dudley nods and smiles. Never growing up is something he can understand.

"You don't grow *up.*" I continue. "You have to grow, though, so you grow upside down or sideways, or twisted in knots like a Bonsai tree, because all these different pressures are always pushing you out of your natural shape. That's why I belong here in this unbearable place, with all these insane rules and people barging in at all hours to check on you and not being allowed to have a key to the street door. The violence and screaming and fighting. It's a day care center for adults. Maybe I'm here because I deserve it."

"Maybe," he says, not really listening, trying to appease me with affirmation. I want to kill him. Kill him and burn the fucking place down. With him in it. With me in it. I'm so furious I don't care.

"Wrong!" I scream, flailing around on the stupid bed. "This is all wrong! This is ridiculous! How can we allow this? How the *fuck* can we allow it?"

"Allow what?" What is she bitching about *now?*

"Jesus," I say. "Never mind."

The Stupid Guy

This stupid guy grows up in the heartland of the homeland. One day Dad sez, Happy Birthday, son! Yer eighteen years old today and there's a *war* going on where you can go fight for yer country just like Good Old Dad did back in '41 before you were even born! And the kid sez, Aww shit, Dad, I don't wanna go fight in no *war*! And Dad sez, That's real stupid, kid.

So Dad rushes into town and signs the kid up to go into the U.S. Army and fight in a good old war just like Good Old Dad did back in '41. Now ya gotta go, ya stupid kid, or they'll put yer stupid ass in jail!! So the stupid guy goes back behind the old barn and picks a hundred pounds of wild marijuana and dries it and cleans it and packs it in nice, neat one-pound packages and takes it to the city and sells it and goes to Berkeley where there are a lot of other stupid guys who don't want to be in the war either.

Pretty soon Dad finds out where the kid is, and he calls the FBI, and the FBI goes and finds the stupid guy hanging around in People's Park and they take him to the Federal Building and put him in jail until the U.S. Army can come and get him.

The U.S. Army comes and gets the guy and takes him to where you get tested before they put you in the Army. They give him an eye test and a foot test and a posture test and lots of other tests and he passes them all pretty well. Then they make him sit at a desk and take an Intelligence Test. The stupid guy fails the test.

The Army doesn't believe that anybody can be stupid enough to fail their Intelligence Test, and they ask the guy if he knows he can get sent to Federal Prison for deliberately pretending to be stupider than he really is on the test. He says no, he didn't know that—he must be pretty stupid. So the Army makes him take a *different* Intelligence Test and he flunks that one too, so the Army decides that this kid is just exactly what he said he was—a totally and abysmally dumb and stupid guy. So they write 4-F on his draft card and say sorry, he can't be in the war because then the whole U.S. Army would have to spend the whole rest of the war running around trying to help this one real stupid guy figure out what to do. So the guy goes back to People's Park and all the other guys say that this is probably the only guy in the history of the universe that ever got four-effed from the U.S. Army just for being stupid.

Now this guy makes $699 a week being stupid. He makes more money in a week than I do in two or three months. He does stupid things in the shipyard. He does things that are so ridiculous that an ordinary person with a brain would never imagine having to do them, and if he did he'd probably run to the nearest window and jump out.

Today the guy comes home from work and he says to the old lady, "Know what happened at work this morning? Some stupid guy drove a fifty-foot crane right off the end of the dock into the bay. It took us four hours to rig up another crane to pull that one out of the bay, and when we did this stupid guy was *still* in there! What a dumb fucker."

Journal Entry: I was looking through the black bag in which I keep odds and ends, mainly pills and empty pill bottles, and thinking that although everything in the bag can be legitimately accounted for, the police would have a lovely time with it.

On the subject of contraband substances, D. asked me to buy him some foot powder after his socks, work boots, and feet developed a sickening aroma after last Tuesday's fourteen-hour shift. To say nothing of huge open sores. I bought a container of foot powder today, which he sprinkled liberally into his work boots upon returning from work. Too liberally. About an ounce went into each boot. To save the excess he dumped it out onto a piece of paper, which he then intended to fold neatly with the powder inside. He looked at the piece of paper with the pile of powder on it and said "I hope the cops don't come in here and find *this*."

4.
The Eviction

Dudley must have known he'd be getting laid off soon after we moved into this place. Laid off, he'd have to wait weeks for his first unemployment check. He'd need good old Ashby to come up with the rent. Of course, he'd also have to put up with her crap, but Ashby's crap is nothing compared to that which they shovel at the homeless shelter.

So he rescued her from the far end of Adeline's couch, where she'd been living with several of Adeline's cats and her asthma inhaler, since being evicted from her residence at The Bunker.

"I went to my own eviction," she'd told Adeline. "I don't know why. I guess I thought I could say something, beg for mercy, or at least listen to what other people were doing so I'd know next time. I never went to Eviction Court before."

"That's rough," says Adeline from the other end of the couch. They're drinking vodka and O.J.

"It was. I was sort of in shock. I was gonna tell the judge how I was sick, and haven't been able to find another place yet, and blah blah blah. The *Judge,* right? He's not gonna toss a sick woman out in the street with no place to go, right? It's like a death sentence, right?" Ashby laughs. "I was so out of touch with real life. I'm sitting in the courtroom for a couple of hours before they call my case. Just me, the judge, and the owner's agent. Two minutes. Boom! You're out. Everybody who showed up in court had maybe two minutes before the judge. They were mostly women, mostly black. The judge has a little hob-nob with the landlord's lawyer and Boom! Next! And these women are all saying 'I been sick' and 'I got no place to go' and 'I got little kids' and Boom! Next! And people were just *stunned*.

"The only person who didn't get evicted that day was a woman who claimed she'd never seen an eviction notice. The landlord's lawyer leaps up. 'You're lying! We served you!! It was delivered to the door of your apartment and *accepted!* You were *served,* Mrs. Blahblah!!'

"'No suh. Never seen it,' says Mrs. B.

'It was delivered to your door.'

'Never seen it.'

'But we got ... but there was ... but we sent three of them at least!'

'No suh, never seen it.'

'Petition for eviction denied,' says the judge. *Next!*

"A minor triumph for all the other potential evictees waiting in the spooky, windowless courtroom. I should have taken the clue. But I'm still living on another planet.

"So the judge says to me, 'Did you receive a notice to Pay Rent Or Quit?'

"And I said 'Yes but. . . .' And the judge says, 'Thirty days to quit the premises.' *Next! Boom!*

"The next woman is instructed to pay three months' rent, and damages. The woman yells, 'I didn't *do* no damages!'

"As I leave the courtroom the landlord's lawyer and the judge are trying to explain to the pissed-off and potentially homicidal woman that 'damages' in Legalese means court costs and lawyers' fees. 'You mean I got to pay for my own eviction?' she yells.

"Yeah, lady. About a thousand bucks."

· · ·

Adeline, listening to all this, just nods and smiles silently.

"I never went to eviction court before," Ashby explains again, trying to excuse her own stupidity. "How many times have *you* been evicted?"

"Maybe eight times," says Adeline.

"Maybe five for me, but I never actually went to court. Just packed up the kids and got out."

"That's all you can do," says Adeline.

"That's not counting the times my parents got evicted when I was a kid."

"Well, now you know," says Adeline. "Never go to court without a lawyer."

"But if I don't have that loot to pay the rent, how'm I gonna afford a lawyer?"

"You got it."

"But I knew that!" Ashby starts laughing. They are both shrieking with laughter. "My parents got evicted when I was four years old! That's more than forty years ago! I knew that!"

"But that was New York, right?" Adeline slugs down a toast. "The good old days. Fucking New York. Never thought California would get *that* bad."

"Oh god."

"So then what?"

"I was crying, kind of groping my way out of the courthouse, trying to figure out how to get out of the building because I couldn't fucking see. I finally get out, and start walking. I was heading toward the estuary because I always home in on the nearest large body of water when I'm hysterical. I got down to Jack London Square, and there's the ferry boat taking on passengers. I had maybe twenty bucks to my name, so I paid the fare and got on the boat. It's a neat boat, kind of jet-propelled. I figured I'd wait until it was out in the middle of the bay, and jump off when nobody was watching."

"Oh honey," Adeline exclaims. "You wouldn't!"

"Yes, I was gonna do it. So I got on the boat and there was this bar. A bar on the boat, so the commuters could get warmed up on their way to work. So I bought a drink and chugged it down. I was looking around, and here were all these fucking commuters, with briefcases open on their laps, trying to get in a little more work before they hit the office. And then there are these tourist types from Shit Creek, taking pictures of the skyline or something, and these healthy hearty young couples in shorts, wheeling bicycles and speaking German and French. So I got another drink. By this time the ferry was stopping in Alameda and all these sailors got on, drinking beer and horsing around. So I drink another drink. I was out on the deck, trying to figure out how to jump. But there were all these tourists and freaks and Navy guys out there too, and there's no way I can jump without somebody seeing me. Besides, I'm having fun. I drink another drink, and I've forgotten about the sheriff and the eviction court and my stuff thrown out in the street. By the time I got to the City, I could hardly walk."

Adeline, by this time, has passed out. Ashby covers her with a blanket and sits back on her end of the couch for a few hours, drinking and crying quietly.

Hermit Crab

Have you ever watched a hermit crab change shells? It outgrows the shell it's living in and has to find a bigger one to occupy. The crab must be completely sure that the new shell is acceptable, and large enough, and uninhabited. Only then will it make the move.

The hermit crab in the process of moving to another shell is possibly the ugliest and most horribly vulnerable creature you'd ever hope to see. And it seems to take forever. You set up the situation, provide the new shell and boil it and sterilize it, and place it right there where the poor guy can't miss it, and you sit without moving, keeping everything warm and quiet, and you still wind up holding your breath for the two hours or whatever it takes to complete the process.

The crab won't even try the move if it feels at risk. But if it doesn't change shells it will die. If the transfer is not successful it will die. It knows this.

People know this, too. But they have to go through with it anyway, when they get evicted or the rent is raised too high for them to pay or some source of income gets lowered or cut off. They do it anyway, and some of them die. A lot of them are able to walk around and feed themselves after they die, but they're still dead. You can tell by looking at the eyes.

5. The Room

The hotel room is average-sized, maybe twelve by fourteen feet. The head of the bed, against which I sit while reading or writing, is against the east wall of the room and a bit right of center. The bed itself is an ordinary double bed, not uncomfortable, mattress and box spring resting on a heavy wooden platform which is impossible to move (and, I suppose, to steal). It has a heavy, solid wood headboard, to which I've attached my reading lamp, but no footboard.

Between the headboard and the wall, in the northeast corner, is a brown-painted wooden nightstand with one small drawer. In the drawer are Dudley's I.D. and other papers, pocket calculator, pen, and flashlight. On top of the stand sits Dudley's clock, ashtray and cigarettes, and a couple of half-burned candles for power failures. Against the north wall, between the stand and the door of the room, an armless chair with brass-colored metal frame and green plastic seat and back.

To my left as I sit against the headboard facing into the room, set into the south wall of the room, a nice-sized window perhaps four feet by five with the sill at knee-level. The window is propped open about eighteen inches from the bottom with half a metal curtain rod wedged into the groove of the frame on either side. A more or less permanent arrangement made by Dudley, who says that the window is extremely heavy to lift due to the counterweights inside the frame being broken off. The lower pane of the window is cracked all the way across and the upper pane cracked across one corner. The cracks have been taped with masking tape, now dry and crumbling. A set of lightweight white curtains hang to the floor, and behind them a plastic window shade on a roller. Between the floor and the windowsill, at the lower right corner of the window, is an old wrought-iron radiator with the adjustment valve taken off and capped.

In the southwestern corner of the room, opposite the foot of the bed on the left, is a shallow niche containing a sink and wooden medicine cabinet with bleary mirror, above which is a light fixture with bare bulb and the only electrical outlet in the room, into which is plugged the extension cord for my reading lamp. The sink's faucets are the kind with springs inside which turn them off when you let go of the handles. Only the cold water works. To the right of this, a tiled shower stall with wooden door, sheet tin nailed on the inside. When turned on, the shower head emits a trickle of water which alternates with alarming frequency between icy cold and blistering hot (when there is hot water at all). To the right of this another door opens into a closet about four feet by five, with shelves along one side. At right angle to the closet is the corridor door on the north wall.

Across from the hall door, on the south wall, stands a rickety wooden dresser with three of its seven knobs missing. On the dresser sits Dudley's old black-and-white TV set, also plugged into the extension cord.

The ceiling height is about ten feet. The ceiling and walls are painted light gray and several cracks run at angles across the ceiling, spackled but not painted. The floor is covered with carpeting of a dark brown, napless indoor-outdoor fiber. There is a hardened, black circular patch between the bed and the window, probably a burn from a hotplate.

The one peculiarity which stands out in my perception of this room is a fuzzy black splotch on the wall about a foot to the right of the door frame. This discoloration is about a foot in diameter, darker at the center and fading out at the edges. After a few days of getting used to the room and its little irregularities—the walled-over outline behind the dresser, which must have once been the door to another room, the lighter patch in the paint of the northeast corner where another piece of furniture must have stood, the cracks in the windows and ceiling hastily and unprofessionally repaired (a banner across the front of the building reads "Grand Opening" and claims a complete renovation since the 1989 earthquake; Dudley says the banner has been there for six months, and it will remain for another six months until shredded by a windstorm in December)—my attention is increasingly drawn to this blotch on the wall. I measure myself against it and see that the center of the blotch is at the approximate height of the center of my head. I note that when the room door is opened inward and I stand behind the opened door, the back of my head is centered within the stain. However, when I stand with my head aligned within the blot, the doorknob of the closed door is more than a foot beyond my reach. Also, that the stain is not a one-time deal, like the bloodstain in the hall toilet. Someone with dirty, greasy hair spent a lot of time standing pressed against the wall in just this position, behind the opened door of the hotel room.

I picture myself as this person, standing behind the door. I'm holding a gun. My partner or roommate is conducting some kind of shady deal in the doorway. Whoever my partner is doing the deal with knows that someone is standing behind the door with a gun. There are no bullet holes in the walls or ceiling.

I explain this scenario to my daughter.

"You've started watching TV again," Jessy says, pleased.

"Take a good look at it." I gesture toward the blot.

Jessy studies the goddamned thing for ten minutes. She studies the door, the doorknob, the ceiling, the walls, the window. She walks to the splotch and stands with her back to the wall. From this position she studies the whole room again. "Jesus," she finally says.

Dudley never notices the spot. He is not terribly perceptive.

Nevertheless, the spot seems to haunt the room. A Mystery Spot.

Money and a Room

If one has no money, one can't very well expect to have a room of one's own, can one? Maybe if one has a BIT of money one can spend it all on rent in order to have a *room* . . . but then it would be just the room, you see, and no . . . OK. What kind of money are we talking about here, and what kind of room? Define your terms. No? OK then, how about just *money?* A room of one's own without money can only be a trap. How can one create anything within a trap that will not be born entrapped?

The animal trapped by the foot will chew off the foot to escape. What about the one who is trapped by the mind? The mind in a trap can't create, it can only stumble around trying to find a way out. And on freeing oneself from one trap, one may find oneself in another, larger trap. Freedom is relative. The bars of the cage may become harder to define. May become impossible to define.

Journal Entry: Went to Martinez today, to the housing authority there, to try to expedite my application for subsidized housing. Another ordeal which could have just as easily been taken care of by mail.

I left the hotel at eleven A.M. and was still fifteen minutes late for my two o'clock appointment. I had enough trouble just trying to find out how to get to the place on BART and bus. People out there don't take busses. They don't understand that it takes an hour on the bus to get someplace that would take ten minutes in a car.

The lady at the housing authority tells me that I need to provide proof that I'm homeless.

"How do you prove that you're homeless?"

The clerk looks up with a puzzled little smile from the pile of paperwork which is supposed to document my financial status, marital status, family status, social status, legal status, educational status, vehicular status, employment status, and the level I have reached in the criminal justice system.

I sense that I'm not going to get a helpful answer. I don't suppose they could just take my word for it.

"I mean," I continue, "All these years I've always had to prove that I lived somewhere. Rent receipts, utility bills, you know. They even come to your place and check, count your kids, the whole bit. I've never had to prove that I didn't live anywhere."

"That's a good question," she says, laughing a little.

"So what do other people do for proof of homelessness?" I'll sign an affidavit. I'll swear to HUD.

"I don't know. We don't have many homeless people in Contra Costa County."

"What would you suggest, then?"

"It's up to *you* to get proof. I just process paperwork. Perhaps a form from a shelter."

"I don't live in a shelter."

She is beginning to show symptoms of exasperation. "Just go in and ask for the form. Surely they'll let you have one."

"I just need the form for the shelter," I say to the woman at the desk at the shelter referral service.

"What form?"

"The form you give someone when you send them to the shelter."

She gives me a funny look. "You want to go to the shelter? There's a waiting list, you know."

"I just want the *form* that says. . . ." I am beginning to sweat all over my laboriously washed sweatshirt. "The referral form."

"You want me to refer you to the shelter."

"That's right."

"Are you homeless?"

"That's right."

"You told me that you are living in the Cracksmoke Hotel on San Pablo."

"I'm getting evicted."

"Where's your eviction notice?"

"I forgot."

"You'll need to bring it in."

"I just want the fu . . . the form. The *form*."

"What do you want the form for?"

"I don't want it. The Contra Costa Housing Authority does."

"What for?"

"Proof that I'm homeless."

"Proof of homelessness? That's the stupidest thing I've ever heard."

"It isn't *my* idea!"

"Look. I don't know what your scam is, but there are people with *real* problems waiting. . . ."

I get up and walk out of the office, crying and formless. Unable to handle going back to my loathsome hotel and my unspeakable room, I find myself sitting in the BART plaza on Fourteenth and Broadway at one o'clock in the morning. Lots of homeless bastards wandering around with filthy blankets wrapped around their shoulders in the shadow of the soaring new American Presidents Lines building. Obviously couldn't do the paperwork necessary to get off the street. How could they if I, with fourteen years of college, can't figure it out?

6.
Real People

Journal Entry: Big moon hanging overhead, will be full on Thursday. One little edge shaved off like a ragged fingernail. Big, eerie, looming. Craziness in the street.

D. was called back to work at the shipyard just in time to screw up his unemployment checks, naturally. A rush job—a week's work at most. Twelve-hour shift yesterday, 4 A.M. to 4 P.M. Today, a fourteen-hour shift, 4 A.M. to 6 P.M. Must get up at 2 A.M. to punch in at 4 in the city. Makes a lot of money, govt. takes most of it because D. has fucked up too many tax returns. (I had to call them, beg them not to take it all.) We could get a real place to live if they didn't have to squeeze so hard. With kitchen and bath. My own kitchen, my own bathroom. Dream on.

Tuesday is Clean Sheets Day at the hotel. I waited around for the Clean Sheets Cart, which showed up around one P.M. Got sheets, pillow-cases, and a roll of t.p. Then I rolled up our blanket and bedspread to take to the laundromat, along with a bag of dirty clothes. Bedspread and blankets have not been washed since we moved in here at the beginning of August. The bedspread was clean then, having been mine, but the blankets probably haven't been washed for years.

The nearest laundromat is about seven blocks away. I didn't know exactly where it was, but I finally found it after walking around for about half an hour. When I got back to the hotel with my clean laundry, all was not right and the Blonde Whore was disclaiming loudly in the lobby. When I made it up to my room (much gasping and panting on the stairs) the B.W. was loudly proclaiming in the street. With her troupe. After this went on for three hours or so without any serious damage inflicted on participants or passersby, I deemed it a pretty good performance.

Jessy comes to visit me in my room a few days later. "Oh, hi, Jessy, how are you?" Dudley says. Without waiting for an answer he retreats into Dudley, who sits staring blankly at the nine-inch screen of his TV.

"Come over here, look at this. You won't believe this." I pull Jessy toward the window.

It is maybe one o'clock in the afternoon, and the street is seething with Street Life. Jessy perches beside me on the bed and we observe the life-forms outside as if they were in an aquarium.

"The window! Look at the window!" In the huge plate glass windows of the office supply store on the other side of the street the front door of the hotel is reflected, four stories below.

"Like in that Tati movie," says Jessy, astonished.

"And I bet me and the guy in the next room are the only ones in the hotel who have this view. It's fucking fantastic."

Winos, whores, derelicts, and drug dealers entering and leaving the hotel are perfectly reflected, in reverse, in the windows across the street.

"It's better than TV!"

"It's perfect!"

A dozen drunks and derelicts, white and black, male and female, are carrying on in the street in front of the hotel. Their base of operations is a concrete tub maybe four feet in diameter, which holds a twelve-foot maple tree, shocked and shuddering but still alive. The winos perch around the edge of the tub, laughing and gesturing, calling to fellow derelicts and harassing passersby, although in a good-natured way, it being a warm easy fall afternoon. They bum cigarettes and spare change for beer, throwing their empties in the gutter, yelling things like "Whooo-Eee!" and "Sheee-It!"

"You think they're nuts now," I say, "wait till the Blonde Whore shows up." She is maybe eighteen or twenty, lives in the hotel when she's not in jail, and indulges in the sort of behavior I have not seen tolerated from anyone else. I call her the Bad News Broad because she is a matrix for violence and mayhem. Every time the Broad sashays into the street, fights break out and screams and curses waft up through the smog. Usually the police have to be called to break up some mini-riot of craziness which is taking place outside and haul at least one person to jail, often the Broad herself. In a day or two she'll reappear, screeching "Hi, honeys! I just got out a jail and I'm back!"

"Wow," Jessy exclaims admiringly. "What's it like out there on Saturday night?"

"Usually pretty quiet. The crazy time is Wednesday, Wednesday night. I figure that by Friday night they're all in jail, or too sick to get out of bed, so weekends are pretty quiet. They let everybody out of jail on Monday, and it takes them until maybe Wednesday afternoon to get totally crazed, so around here Wednesday night is the big one."

"Patterns," says Jessy, "are being altered everywhere. Like a Tati movie."

"But didn't Tati believe in the essential goodness of mankind?"

"Don't worry," says my daughter, "You taught me better than that."

Sometimes while street-watching we concentrate on the "real people." Downtown office workers and business people, employees from the civic center or the library or the main post office, civil servants. When the weather is nice, Jessy will bring her lunch down from the office where she works farther uptown to observe the ongoing war between the street people and the Real People. She enjoys anticipating how a woman in very high heels will react to an empty beer can or wine bottle rolling across the sidewalk. She cheers at the verbal skirmishes which occur when a Real Person loses control in the midst of a chorus of "Gimme a cigarette" and "Gimme a quarter!"

"Culture shock!" she yells. "Get the Wino Wagon!"

For several weeks a mounted cop has made the hotel part of his regular beat. The winos shuffle off in different directions when hoof-beats are heard. Then the city removes the concrete planter, tree and all. The winos move on to other turf. Just as well. Their goofy and inarticulate rage was getting boring; violence was building up. The Real People take back the street.

"Don't you want to be a Real Person when you grow up?" I ask Jessy one day.

"There are no Real People," she says.

There was a time when I thought I could become a real person with a real job. Like when I finally got my high school diploma, fifteen years too late. That didn't work, so I went to junior college, then Real College. After fourteen years of college and nine-tenths of an MFA, still no Real Job.

I was living with Jessy in The Bunker, where we relocated from student housing. As soon as we got settled in that tiny space, I told her: "Now I'm going to go get a job!"

She fell over laughing. "Oh Mom! Nobody is going to give *you* a job!"

"Yes they will," I said firmly. "I'm going to look for one. What'll I wear?"

So I spent about six months trying to figure out how to get an outfit of clothes in which to apply for a job. Just *one* outfit would be enough to get started. Jessy was no help, aside from brightening the atmosphere with volleys of laughter at frequent intervals. Eventually, I managed to get a department store credit card. On the application, I wrote some things which could be interpreted as not exactly the truth.

I spent several weeks thinking about how I was going to go shopping with my new card. Then I gave up.

I came to the realization that I didn't know how to dress. The area with which Americans are most familiar, shopping, was a mystery to me. I knew nothing about clothes. These things do not come naturally—they are Learned Behavior.

"You're right," I told Jessy. "I may as well have spent my life in a locked closet in the loony bin."

I gave her my card. She bought me a T-shirt, sweat pants, and a pair of Nikes.

Cat Star

One evening I was staring out at the freeway, leaning on my windowsill in The Bunker, and I noticed a flattened-out shape in the middle of the street beneath my window, on westbound MacArthur Boulevard. The Bunker was supposed to be an apartment, at least the landlord called it one, which composed the upper story of a two-story structure made of concrete blocks. The lower part was a tiny storefront, unoccupied at that time. Designed to recall the cheap-motel school of architecture from the fifties, this building was tacked onto the front of a wooden bungalow which rented as a separate unit. The Bunker occupied what had once been the bungalow's front yard.

The window overlooked about fifteen lanes of traffic, interrupted by median strips of shrubbery and weeds, which included the 580 freeway, two off-ramps and an on-ramp, separating the east-and-west-bound halves of MacArthur Blvd. with its underpasses and overpasses and a sidewalk somewhere for pedestrians.

And here was a shape in the middle of MacArthur in front of my window, a five-pointed star which turned out on closer inspection to be the four legs and tail of a cat. The cat's head was just a blob between two of the points. It was totally splayed out like a cartoon animal that had had a grand piano dropped directly on its head from a great height. I wondered if the cat had been shot, either by the heads in the crack-house next door or by one of the Freeway Snipers the cops were always after, maybe during the morning's four A.M. lull in traffic. Maybe it had strayed into the line of fire at the Seven-Eleven on the corner, which was always being robbed and shot at. I finally decided, on further contemplation, that the cat had been flattened by a speeding bus, either the 57, the 34 or the N San Francisco, all of which ran under my window after clearing the underpass down the hill.

I hoped that the cat had belonged to someone on my side of the freeway. To have made it across fourteen lanes from the other side, and then get nailed six feet from the curb, was too monstrous to think about.

The day after I first noticed the Cat Star, it started to rain. Just a miserable gray drizzle, which can go on for weeks in the winter in northern California. It started washing away little bits and pieces of the Star. I started noticing how many cars actually went by in the street outside, as opposed to the tens of thousands on the freeway. I started to notice how very few pedestrians walked by. I noticed how the bus drivers all stomped on their gas pedals right under my window. I noticed that I felt dizzy a lot. I noticed that most of the people on the block never opened their windows.

The Cat Star kept getting wider and more flattened-out during the next few days, like a pie crust under grandma's rolling pin. It wasn't bloody or gross or anything, because the rain washed away the bodily fluids. It was mainly skin and fur after a couple of days. I avoided looking out the window whenever I could, and when I did look out I forced my attention toward the freeway with only a split-second glance to see what was happening to the Cat Star under my window.

It took a week of miserable drizzling rain, and busses and trucks and cars, to erase all traces of the Cat Star. I was glad when it had finally vanished without a trace. I tried to erase it from my memory, but that didn't work as well.

I still have this Cat Star somewhere in my head.

7.
The Doomed

Dudley's employers never tell him when he's going to be laid off until the last minute. He'll get his pink slip and last paycheck at the end of the shift. I don't understand how his employers can be allowed to get away with this. What does the union say about it? Dudley just shrugs. It's standard procedure everywhere. I still don't believe it.

Dudley is working swing shift when he gets laid off, and usually gets back to the hotel at 1:30 A.M. This time, he comes in at seven A.M., totally wiped out. He is black from head to foot, his clothes, hair, and face covered with black grease and soot except for white rings around the eyes where his safety goggles had been. His face looks like a negative of a raccoon, and he stinks of fuel oil and smoke. His eyes aren't in focus.

"I worked six hours overtime, and I got laid off." He says nothing more. He peels off his stiffened work clothes and puts them in a plastic trash bag. He gets in the shower and scrubs for half an hour. His hair is still greasy when he gets out, climbs into the bed and goes to sleep without another word.

Outside, I can already see smog layering itself between the

buildings. Dudley sleeps the sleep of the dead. I hate him. The room stinks of petroleum products and the rotting leather of his work boots. I have to get out.

In the lobby, zombified people sit and watch the TV screen. Dudley has told me that these are mental patients released into the "community," which doesn't want them. I call them The Doomed. Some of them wear layers of woolen clothes, gloves, and hats, even in the warmest weather. Maybe it's the drugs they take. They stare at the TV all day, watching whatever is playing, and don't seem to notice when the channel is changed. The State sends their rent checks directly to the hotel.

The coffee machine and the Coke machine are out of order. The Desk Guy glares blearily out from behind the desk, waiting for someone to give him an excuse to be mean and ugly. The pay phone is being hogged by a drug dealer, who alternately whispers and shouts into it.

"I tol' you, nothin's happenin' right now. . . ." he bursts out. Then more quietly "Usual place . . . show the green . . . maybe an hour. . . ." Cryptic stuff. Little rat-faced white guy, probably a cop. Not exactly professional, being such a pain in the ass. I should think one would want to be more subdued, more anonymous. . . .

The atmosphere outside is foul as well, but not as bad as back in the room. I should just go get a bottle of wine, forget it. The hotel winos already have their first hooch of the day, but most of them just drink Green Mamba or, at worst, Frisco, a sort of alcoholic Kool-Aid. You can see them out at six in the morning waiting for the corner store to open, so they can start getting through the day, score whatever it is that gets them through, unlike The Doomed who only take the drugs that the doctor ordered.

I don't want to go out into the cruel world, the street. I should sit down with The Doomed and watch TV with them, and allow myself to feel the rage they're not allowed to feel. But what if I am really no better than they are, and can't handle it either?

. . .

Prisoners of Gravity

Ashby, a prisoner of gravity, drags herself up the stairs in the transient hotel (wrong name for the place because nobody in here is going anywhere except maybe to jail, the nuthouse, or the cemetery.)

Drooling mental patients with blank faces sit in the lobby all day, grounded out by Thorazine, staring at the TV. (*The Flintstones Sesame Street* soap opera *The Brady Bunch* golf.) Signed a waiver to life and future, nailed down to the most dismal reality unimaginable. Just harmless nuts you see until one day one of them forgets to take her pill and turns the set into something resembling Godzilla trashing Tokyo. Nice little old lady, too—she smiles at Ashby sometimes on the stairs.

Poor fuckers can't handle psychosis, so it's no fun for them. With all activity centers and sensory apparatus shorted out by Haldol it takes two hours to tie your shoes.

"I see awful things, Doc." The shrink writes PATIENT HALLUCINATING on the chart and gives a prescription for Thorazine every four hours which turns the brain right off. Patient goes "home" to transient hotel in the neighborhood where people are dying in doorways slow suicide instant suicide you can buy it on the corner muggings rape torture knives bullets police kick down the door wrecked car upside down on the sidewalk home to a family of four. Sit down in the lobby nailed down to watch patterns of violence on the TV. Waived his right to life.

The Yuppie Psychologist patiently explains to the Baglady: "When you drink alcohol, you are anesthetizing yourself and repressing your feelings of anger."

BAGLADY: "Is that bad?"

YUP: "Of course it's bad! You must let your angry feelings come *out!*"

Ashby laughs. "But the last time I did that I wound up in jail and tried to kill myself."

Ashby dragging herself up the stairs to her room in the transient hotel. Phoneless room—none of the rooms have phones or even phone jacks and there is only the pay phone in the lobby for drug dealers. She clutches a list of phone numbers from the Free Mental Health Clinic:

"Of *course* we can help you!" Call this number—free—24-hour Mobile Psychological Crisis Unit *call* 24-hours *day or night* if you can find a pay phone that works in that godawful neighborhood where you live while in the middle of a psychotic break.... (Psychosis breaks out in Ashby, drug dealers are waiting on line for the phone in the lobby so she goes out into the dark streets look for a pay phone and there is one two blocks away which silently swallows her quarter and refuses to give it back. Two more blocks this phone screeching helplessly in static and the next block's phone is missing many vital parts so she pulls out of her Baglady bag the softball-sized piece of granite carries for self-defense screaming and cussing pounds the hopeless instrument into flying chunks while a wino lying in the next doorway cheers and applauds "Thas right! Lettum have it, baby!")

So it's true that just when you think things are as bad as they can get, they get worse. Now that Dudley's laid off, I'll have to spend 24 hours a day trying to put up with him. His complaints, his snoring, his "reading," his watching TV with the sound turned up because he's deaf. The Doomed are better off. At least they have their own rooms and their prescribed drugs. To be able to make the world go away. To be entertained by TV! To tell the world to fuck off! What is the *world*, anyway? What is *life?* Have you had your psychotic break today?

Journal Entry: I went down to Hayward on BART yesterday, to the Alameda County Social Services main office, to try to get help with verification of homelessness. I finally got to talk to a worker on the house phone. Women were standing on line behind me juggling screaming babies, waiting to use the phone. The worker said she couldn't help me. I talked very fast, very reasonable and articulate. She couldn't help. She couldn't give me anything to verify homelessness. She couldn't understand why anyone would require such a thing. She must have thought I was crazy. She wouldn't see me in person, wouldn't even give me her name. They must have to deal with a lot of desperate people who take this stuff personally.

8. Alarms

Journal Entry: At this point in my life I feel that there's not much I can do which would be considered acceptable, but to whom and for what reasons I don't know. It's difficult to make the smallest decision. The bottom drops out; I'm faced with the Void.

Wasn't I always the one who never worried about doing the unacceptable thing, or was that part of my false image? My identity is slipping, I'm seeing myself more and more through the eyes of others. I worry about trying to do what is expected of me. Even though I don't really know exactly what's expected of me I hate myself for not having lived up to anyone's expectations. I don't even know what I expected of myself. Haven't I learned *anything?*

The utility company seems to have finished tearing up the street below my window, so the external noise level has gone back to almost bearable. Is this what they mean by "being able to hear oneself think"?

I wake up every morning between three and four A.M. and spend a couple of hours at the typewriter inside my head. Whether or not anything meaningful is being produced I don't know, but it seems to put some distance between me and the Pit.

Between the boredom and the violence there's not much. After a few weeks the violence becomes predictable and then boring. On our floor of the hotel we know who the guy is who beats up his girlfriend, and the homosexual who locks his lover out of the room. The cries of the lover, begging and pleading in the hall, the cries of the beaten girl, who works nights as a nurse's aide. She's black, so the bruises don't show and she goes off to work crying and bruised and the next day she's back with her boyfriend, who is white and on parole for all kinds of hideous behavior, and runs around waving his gun in the hall when he's stoned. And the old drunk who collects cans and cries and prays loudly in his room alone.

The police come through banging on doors, looking for some criminal or other.

BangBangBang.

"Who is it?"

"Police. Open up."

Open the door. They don't come in the room. They're afraid to come in these rooms.

"We're looking for Jeffrey. Jeffrey live here? Where is he?"

"No sir, no Jeffrey here. I'm Dudley. Wanna see my I.D.? This is my girlfriend Ashby. Wanna see her I.D.? No Jeffrey here, officer. Wrong room, officer sir."

"Sorry. We hadda complaint. We hafta check."

"Right right, officer. Right. My I.D., see? This is me. I live here with my girlfriend. No Jeffrey here, sir, officer. OK?"

"Sorry. We hadda check it out. We hadda complaint. Wrong room. Right. Sorry. Have a nice day."

One time they come through with dogs. Dope-sniffing dogs. Went through every room, sniffing. Busted everybody with drugs.

TENANT: "Where'd *that* stuff come from? That ain't *my* stuff! What *is* that stuff, anyway? Not mine, officer sir! I just moved in an hour ago. Guy left it who lived here before, probly. Right? Guy just moved out, leaves his stuff, right?"

COP: "Right. Assume the position."

TENANT: "Who, *me?* Listen, I don't do that stuff. I just smoke *pot,* right? Whatever that stuff is. I only smoked a joint, OK? I don't hafta go to jail for that! I don't even got any left! This other guy who lived here before I moved in, right? Right?"

"Shut up, asshole. You're goin' down."

A VOICE DOWN THE HALL: "Hey, man—I'm just a drunk, see? I *drink,* right? It's legal ta *drink,* right? I'm fifty years old, I gotta right, I gotta right ta get drunk, right? I don't smoke nunna that stuff. Whatever it is I didn't smoke it, man. I'm just a drunk, right? Ya see all these empty bottles?"

The Fire Department barges in with no grace at all. There was a fire in the hotel around the corner a few months ago. Top two floors totally burned out, killed some unidentifiable people. Dudley was living there then, on the second floor. They evacuated the place while it burned, but then they had all these decrepit stoned people standing around in the street with no place to go, so they let them go back to their rooms. Dudley went back to his room, went to bed, and the ceiling fell on his head. The water which the Fire Department had poured into the top floors of the building soaked down through the ceiling of the room where Dudley was asleep and it fell on him and knocked him out.

He wakes up in an ambulance parked in front of the hotel.

"Are you OK, sir?"

"Yeah, I'm OK."

"You wanna go to the hospital?"

"No, I'm OK."

"Are you *sure* you're OK?"

"Yeah, I'm OK."

So Mr. Patel, the manager of the hotel, pays him $200 to sign a release, and tells him to go around the corner and give the $200 to Mr. Patel, the manager of this other hotel. And he does.

"What an idiot!!" His girlfriend screams and beats her head on the wall when she hears this stupid story. "You could have sued them!

You could have got lots of loot! You coulda got a room at the Hyatt Regency!"

"But I'm *already* brain damaged," says Dudley. "I was brain damaged way before the ceiling fell on my head."

"Obviously," she says. Then she moves in with him.

It was around eleven P.M. when the Fire Department came thundering through the halls of this hotel. I tried to wake Dudley up but he told me to fuck off. So I ran out into the smoke-filled hallway to see what was going on. The fire was on the floor above us. Some tenants had tried to drag the fire hose from our floor up the stairs because there's no hose up there. This is your standard heavy canvas hose with the brass nozzle, supposed to be one hanging on the wall on every floor. So these drunks drag the goddamned thing up there and then find out it doesn't work, is completely useless. And here come the firemen in their rubber coats yelling "Get out of here!! What's wrong with you people? You deserve to roast in this shit!"

It turned out to be a garbage-can fire. Probably set by some pissed-off tenant or ex-tenant. It's so easy.

But this choking smoke is everywhere, so I go out and sit on the sidewalk in front of the hotel. Sitting next to me is the maid who cleans all the toilets in the hotel. She's young, black, and missing a lot of teeth. Her boyfriend is sitting on the curb looking even younger, and very paranoid. I ask her if she gets free rent for cleaning out all the toilets in the hotel every day. She laughs. "Hell no! Are you *kidding?*"

The boyfriend asks me if I'm a cop. My turn to laugh. He stalks away, saying he's going to feed the ducks in Lake Merritt. The maid has a tall can of Green Mamba. I have half a bottle of wine. We sit there mumbling in the dark until Mr. Patel the manager comes out and tells us "Eet ees so rude to seet like zees in zee street." He looks at his gold watch and orders us to our rooms.

"My room is full of smoke," I say. "Go to hell."

He goes away.

· · ·

The owners of the Sleaze Hotel seem to want to populate their establishment with corpses who will remain inanimate in their rooms, in the dark, indefinitely, without eating or drinking or evacuating or even sweating (thus eliminating the necessity for clean sheets, light bulbs, toilet paper). The sole function of these "tenants" would be to once a week somehow make it down to the desk and pay their rent.

The owners of all sleazy hotels and motels seem to be named Patel, and they are all from India. They hate us, and look upon us as slime. For all I know, they think all Americans are slime. Then again, this may just be the rationalization they use in order to abuse and exploit us without mercy. Yet they expect us to be clean and quiet, show respect, and give them all our money.

They get angry when their expectations fall outside the realm of possibility, and seem to live in a constant boiling rage because of this, stalking to and from the hotel and their other shady enterprises in the neighborhood, their gold watches flashing in the sun. They take their anger out on the tenants whenever they can.

Here's some poor guy coming home from his lousy job, creeping up the stairs with his six-pack. The Patel comes bounding out of his office: "You! You owe me rent! You don't pay the rent three weeks! Where's the money?"

GUY: "Uh ... I paid my rent. It's paid up. Maybe the Desk Guy made a mistake."

OWNER: "No mistake! You owe rent money! Pay now or get out!"

GUY: "I gotta receipt."

OWNER: "You in 612, right? Three weeks you owe!"

GUY: "No, I'm in 204. I paid. I gotta receipt."

OWNER: "You 204?"

GUY: "That's right."

OWNER: "I thought you 612. OK. You paid, OK. Sorry."

GUY: "Asshole."

How much of this can you take? Everyone has their limits. After a while you want to just wrap that gold watch around their neck.

"But they have this shit list, Ash," Dudley says. "All the hotels have a copy. You fuck up, get on the list, you won't get a room anywhere."

"So?"

"So then it's the shelter circuit. After that, the street."

"I've been in the street."

"Yeah, in the sixties. The good old days."

"The good old days of the Street. It was bad, but it wasn't really mean. The street I grew up on was worse than this, but it wasn't as *mean*."

"The good old days."

"The good old Street days."

"Fucking right."

"You have a bad attitude. You have a *terrible* attitude, Ash."

"Fucking right."

"You see?"

"Justice and Liberty, Dud. Liberty and Justice. And the Pursuit of Happiness."

"You're nuts," he says, turning to face the wall. "Just shut up with your Liberty shit. I'm not gonna let you get *me* in trouble with that shit."

She lies quiet for a long time, then recites: "They can poke a tube right into my stomach, pump food right in, and wine, so I won't complain, and put an I.V. right in my arm and pump in the drugs, so I won't complain. And stick a tube in my bladder, and one up my ass, to suck out the waste products. And periodically They can disconnect me from the machines so I can get my check from the mailbox and cash it and pay the rent the rent the rent. And then They can drag me back and hook me up again. But I'd probably fight. 'Cause I have a baaaad attitude." She looks at Dudley. He is dead asleep.

Journal Entry: I had a dream that my body was an enormous box, open on top, made of heavy wood or concrete like a dry-dock, and it was gradually being poured full of cement. I am the box, lying on my back looking up, feeling the cement fill me up.

9. Life Forms

I have been told that the word "carnival" comes from the Latin word meaning "meat." A lot of people get together and eat meat. Maybe in prehistoric times when they killed a large animal they all got together and ate and partied until it was gone. A tribal thing. They were forced to share because they had no refrigeration, or maybe it didn't occur to them to do otherwise.

Anyway, there are these urban carnivals, which come around to the Inner Cities and set up for a week in some school yard or parking lot. People get together to devour each other.

The equipment is brought in on flatbed trucks. The "rides," unassembled, are piles of steel framework, I-beams, cables, painted bright colors. They assemble the things by bolting them together. Each one is run by a big electric generator and all the generators run off of a master generator, and there are these big electric cables snaking all over the ground everywhere. They also have "booths" where they have knock-over-the-lead-bottles games, and puncture-the-balloon games, and toss-a-dime-into-the-dish games, and stuff like that. If you win, you get a plastic key-ring or something.

Dudley wanted to take me to one of these affairs. He didn't want to go alone, so I went with him. He had never been to one of these inner city junk carnivals before. They are designed for the urban poor who have no access to places like Disneyland and Great Flags and Ocean World. They attract the children, with a barrage of bright lights and loud noises impossible to ignore in the ghetto, and the parent who doesn't come up with at least one handful of loot for their kid to spend at this event is doomed to burn in hell for quite a while—maybe forever.

I had attended these things before—they haven't changed much since I was a child. We went on some of the "rides." A few beers and a joint beforehand helped a bit. Dudley won me some goldfish by tossing dimes into their bowls; I put them in a jar to turn loose in the Oakland Museum fishpond. Where they'd probably get eaten by turtles, but at least have a few moments of relative freedom first.

After dark, the scene was illuminated in the red glow of lights reflected by low clouds. A lurid light. Most of the children had been taken home, and the older people were starting to wonder if they'd had any fun yet. Wandering around looking for the fun they'd told themselves they were going to have. The whole place was on the edge of violence waiting to break out, and groups of angry, cheated teenagers were prowling the perimeters looking for a victim or a fight.

At the entrance to one of the rides I walked into a crowd of twenty or thirty people who were witnessing an event. These were mainly tired adults, tired not only of the carnival but of whatever had brought them there.

The operator of the "ride," one of those contraptions which spins around and turns upside down, was trying to get a woman off of the machine. He was a young kid, a teenager, who didn't speak English very well. The customer was a belligerent drunk woman of maybe thirty, who didn't want to get off the ride. The main problem was that she had her baby with her, a baby too young to know what was going on, and the baby was terrified. It seemed that she had already been on the ride four or five times with the baby, which was now screaming and thrashing in convulsions of terror. It had puked all over itself and Mom, some bright orange chemical goo which was soaking into the front of Mom's clothes, and was obviously out of control. The woman was extremely drunk.

MOM: "I wanna go again. I got tickets. I bought tickets" (waving a handful of tickets) "and I gotta right. I wanna go again. I wanna."

OPERATOR: "Look, lady, iss no good. The kid he's scared. You wanna go home."

MOM: "Hell no! I gotta right. I paid for tickets. I wanna ride." Clutching the screaming vomiting kid to her chest. "Here's a ticket! I wanna ride some more."

The crowd is silent, watching. Hopeless. Somebody says "The poor kid." Meaning the baby or the operator, no one can tell.

Somebody else in the crowd says "Get her offa there."

The crowd is tense, but tired. Nobody knows what to do. "Call the cops," somebody suggests.

"I wanna ride again. I gotta ticket," the woman yells. Other people are getting impatient, waiting to ride. The baby screams.

Someone in the crowd says "This ain't human. This ain't even fuckin real."

"Yeah it is," says somebody else.

The operator gives up, goes back to his control box, and Mom and baby are whirled up out of sight.

"This is shit!" says someone.

The crowd disperses, wandering away in different directions, soon distracted by bright lights and sounds.

Journal Entry: When I decided at a very early age to become an observer, I didn't realize that it was something you had to keep working on forever. The only way to become a real master of observation is to observe yourself in the process of observing and to try not to pass judgement on whatever is being observed. You may pass judgement on yourself, but only in the form of constructive criticism aimed at your capacities as an observer.

I've observed that people in the street seeing me in my present bag lady form don't believe that I'm a real person. At least not real in the same sense that they are real. To them I seem to appear as perhaps a symptom of urban blight, or the ills of society, or maybe just a vague threatening figure from some nightmare.

If I try to talk to them they will not hear what I say, because I am unreal to them. They see an image. To be recognized in my role I must ask for spare change or a cigarette, or spout obscenities, or exhort about Jesus, and thus become classifiable. What I really want to do is explain how I came to be in this uncomfortable and inconvenient position, but that would take years. I'm sure that all the Real People out there would much rather just give me a quarter or a cigarette.

I've been eating at St. Vinnie's Free Dining Room every day. Beans, macaroni, macaroni, beans. Canned peach shreds, half a hot dog bun. Veggies rarely. A couple of days ago, cold broccoli mush with bacon grease on it. Lots of little kids and pregnant women there today. Macaroni with something that was probably supposed to have been cheese, peach shreds, a little chunk of poisonous yellow squash. We thank thee, O Lord.

Journal Entry: Spent half the night sitting in the plaza by the 12th St. BART station, talking to the mice, feeding them crumbs from the bottom of my bag. I don't know how I got to the plaza, but I vaguely remember why I got thrown out of the hotel. I must have been too drunk to make it up the stairs (the elevator being out of order as usual) and fallen asleep sitting in the lobby. This is against the rules. The next thing I remember is being out in the street with the doors being locked behind me.

No point in getting angry, violent; just go somewhere and cool off until the next shift takes over the desk. You see, officer, I'm not a criminal—I have a place to live. Here's my room key, see? Just a peaceful harmless bag lady out to get some fresh air, OK?

And I've always been nice to mice, though I don't suppose one gets any points for that.

Slow death in the street. What do we think about, sitting out there in the dark, with Death hanging out on every street corner? What would *you* think about? You could be anybody's victim, fair game and easy prey. Used for target practice. Who would protect you, who would miss you, who would demand justice? The kick in the ribs, the blow on the head, broken nose and knocked-out teeth. Some stranger, pissed off about something.

And if and when you recover from the shock, you find out that they've taken your blanket and your cigarettes, your gloves and your ratty old knitted cap and your bag with all the stuff you needed to survive: flashlight and extra socks and your I.D. and your pills (because you're *always* sick) and whatever money you had and even the book you were reading to pass the time (the dumb and stupid Time you have to spend sitting on some bench waiting for something to happen . . . maybe something *good* . . . ?) and your soap and towel and toothbrush and comb or whatever you use to try to keep from looking like a total wreck.

There's a feeling of deep horror, which one must set aside in order to be able to function at all. Fear is a condition which one can't set aside because it is essential to one's survival. To offset the fear, one must always keep the anger burning. These two elements are what keeps one going, but neither must be allowed to overcome the other.

Crouching at the base of some steel-and-glass cliff in some deserted downtown area—deserted except for other human debris such as yourself—in the middle of the night, talking to the mice, hoping that their prayers and squeaks of thanks might be heard by some god putting in a good word on your behalf. Hoping for some barely imaginable terminal event whereby you and all your rodent pals will arrive simultaneously at heaven's gate with no excuses needed. I feel like I've lost my dreams, but I've only really lost what I could have been under better circumstances. And I'm stuck between that and whatever I will become, which could be someone's worst nightmare for all I know.

The afternoon guy must have said something to the night guy at the desk, because I get this *look*, this reluctant-to-be-mean, semi-sympathetic glare from the night Desk Guy as he unlocks the door for me. Are you gonna be a Good Girl? Am I gonna be sorry for letting you back in? Smile and shrug. It's Check Day, you know? I got a little high, but I paid my rent first, OK? You know how it is, right?

Yes, he knows *exactly* how it is.

OK, so I talk to mice, but I always speak politely, perhaps even conspir-atorially. You might happen to observe me doing this and assume that I'm talking to myself, or to Jesus, or perhaps even to *you*, but this is not the case.

I also occasionally talk to pigeons, seagulls, cats, insects, and trees. Sometimes they seem to be listening. When I talk to people, they never listen. When I talk to myself, I don't listen.

I think that talking to lower life forms (or perhaps higher—who knows?) may be a form of prayer, but one can never be sure. Better just to fantasize that the pigeon, waiting for the next crumb with its stupid little beady head cocked to one side, is listening.

It seems that appearances still count. When one starts worrying about how one might look to mice and other small animals, I think it's safe to say that we must all appear the same to them: a huge, threatening mountain of flesh, carnivorous flesh, to whom *you* might appear only as a tasty tidbit.

When I walk through the hotel lobby I can see myself peripher-ally in a series of staggered flashes in the mirrored panels which were left after the earthquake of '89, and I seem to look no better or worse than I've ever looked—baggy sweatpants and sweatshirt, dirty old run-ning shoes, long hair and sunglasses covering as much of the face as possible. Big ragged purse; the bag lady's Bag.

I was never young, therefore I will never be old. A comforting thought.

I am not "old" in the American sense: the bonds maturing, the kids out of college, the retirement checks impending, the house paid for, the kids out of the army, the travel brochures in the mailbox, the condo in Miami. The spreading cancer, the clogged arteries, the triple-bypass surgery, the face-lift, the tummy-tuck, the bifocals, the dentures. None of these things loom over my shoulder, therefore I'm not Old.

If I can reasonably say that I'm not old, I can also say that I am not young. I am not anything. I don't have a part to play out in the American nightmare. I can do anything, be anybody. I don't have to dress up. Like a child, I could put on wobbly high heels and a dress (somebody's dress) a hat, maybe dab on rouge and lipstick, paint the eyes, pin up the hair in some form or another, drape cheap jewelry around the neck and from the ears, carry a purse. Find a nice little white purse to carry my shit around in. Look like a real person. A hat with fake flowers. Go to church on Sunday in this drag. Pray. In grownup drag. Pretend to be somebody.

In a short year's time I'd come to this place full of hopeless, defeated people from a place full of young, energetic, healthy people for whom hope was not even an issue. Actually, hope was not an issue with the defeated group either because they had none. On campus, everyone seemed to be stuffed with assurances and assumptions. They took everything for granted, from indoor plumbing and running water to perfect teeth and perfect health to high-paying jobs and owning a house and getting all the good things life had to offer. Because they knew that all the good things were accessible to them. Is it just a matter of accessibility then? Do all Americans have the right to life, liberty, and blah blah blah, or is this a children's fantasy, like Santa Claus? Everyone has access to college, don't they? (Dudley: "If they let *you* in, they'd let *anybody* in.") And through college, access to all the other goodies, right?

How I beat myself with this thought, night after night, trying to fall asleep in the Hopeless Hotel. You had access to the goodies and you blew it, didn't you? But how, exactly, did I blow it? When? Or even more relevant: why? I certainly had hope when I arrived at school, fresh from forty years of a hopeless life. I was going to totally change my life, I hoped. But hope wasn't good enough. It was only good enough for those who didn't need it. Those who were confident and assured.

And I realized that hope wasn't a reasonable premise to operate on. Any idiot can have hope. A beaten child or a beaten dog can always hope that it won't be beaten again. But that doesn't work; hope doesn't make it happen. If you are a beaten dog, you go out and beat up a smaller dog. If you are a beaten child you grow up, have your own kids, and beat *them*. The point being, you have to recognize the difference between how They say things are supposed to work, how you think things are supposed to work, and how things really work. This takes work.

Between the cloying self-esteem of the academic community and the abyss of the Derelict Hotel I had my year in The Bunker, which served as a buffer zone. Without that, I know I would have skidded a lot closer to the edge than I did. Too suddenly, it would have been like a thousand-foot fall without a parachute, and the laws of acceleration would have killed me.

So when Dudley helped me carry my stuff on the bus down to our new home in the hotel, I was thinking: "This is a perfect excuse to start over. I'll see what I can do with one bag of clothes, a bedspread, two towels, a lamp, a notebook, and my copy of *Gravity's Rainbow*. I'll begin anew."

I thought the hotel room bleak and gloomy beyond description (read description). Chokingly dusty. The bedspread tattered and filthy (I replaced it with mine). I hung up my reading lamp. There was a shower stall in the room, the size of an ordinary closet, tiled on the inside. We paid maybe $20 extra per week to have our own shower. I scrubbed out the wastebasket in the room, which was an empty five-gallon paint bucket, and used it to wash my clothes in, in the shower. We also pissed in the shower stall, because the toilet down the hall was usually filthy.

Sometimes I would spend hours in the shower. I would be a peasant woman scrubbing the laundry on the banks of the river. I would wash my hair four or five times. I'd scrub the tiles one by one. After washing my clothes I hung them in the window to dry. This is a common practice in sleazy hotels. With only an hour or so of sunlight, it would take at least two days for heavy items like socks and sweatshirts to dry. I didn't have many clothes, and the ones I had were ragged, but they were always clean. I wanted to always be clean. It made me feel better.

Sometimes I'd ride the bus past the Scum Of The Earth Hotel, which was a lot worse than our hotel. This hotel had an armed guard in the lobby at all times and a locked gate at the stairway and no pay phone, and was possibly the worst hotel in the East Bay. (But I'd visited a friend there one time and her room had a smashing view of the Bay and the Golden Gate.) Passing this hotel on the bus, I'd always see clothes drying in the windows. In one window there were always children's clothes. The mother of the kids was trying to keep their clothes clean using the same methods as I: washing them in a bucket and hanging them in the window to dry. This involves exhausting effort. This woman will spend a whole day doing what the middle-class housewife can do in half an hour. And does she get credit for this effort? Not likely. She'll get the "what kind of a mother *are* you" speech from the social workers and schoolteachers, "What kind of a mother would bring children up in such a place, without a washer-dryer?" Ragged children's clothes hanging in the window drying and displaying to the world your failure as a mother.

Journal Entry: Check Day has come and gone, people have paid their rent and have some left over. Early in the morning when the corner store opens they're out buying their first tall can of Green Mamba. A bit shocking to see a pregnant woman drinking G.M. for breakfast, more shocking because I could easily see myself doing it if I thought I had dead-ended in this ghastly place.

Most of these people seem pretty badly damaged. They're granted the freedoms and responsibilities of a seven-year-old. If they were given more responsibility, they'd fuck it up, of course. Don't most of us feel compelled to do what is expected of us?

So, *be* a martyr!

Wallow in filth and sleep on broken glass if it gives you some satisfaction.

Some sick satisfaction!

(Not implying that *you* should do it, of course, so what's the threat?)

Ascetics of all nations, beware!

What is Health Insurance, anyway? Does it insure that you'll be healthy, or does it make you feel a little sicker? What if only the healthy can get it? Do these people know what health *is*? Does life insurance guarantee you a life? Do They know what life is? Is this *It*?

Are these people homeless and rejected because they're damaged, or are they damaged because they've been rejected and are homeless?

Has the law of cause and effect broken down?

What law of cause and effect?

11.

Conversations

Conversation overheard on the back of the 57 bus, the day after Halloween:

TEENAGE GIRL: "I got my trick and my treat last night. Yeah, I got my treat. And I got my trick.

"I been smokin joints all day. Smokin and smokin and smokin.

"I'm gonna hafta go to jail."

TEENAGE BOY: "For how long?"

GIRL: "About a year. Darleen got eleven months."

BOY: "Didn't your mama get the same thing?"

GIRL: "I dunno . . ."

I am reading, on my side of the bed near the window, holding up the paperback book to catch the light from the reading lamp.

Outside in the evening of the street, the raucous voice of the Blonde Whore can be heard whooping and wheedling and trying to encourage a fight among the tub-sitters. Six or seven other voices can be heard whoo-eeing and gaw-damning from time to time. Angry voices flare up and die out amidst drunken laughter.

"Gaw-Dammmm!" somebody yells.

"Hon-Neeee!" screeches the Blonde Whore.

I lower my book, distracted. "She *has* to be an undercover cop. Trying to drum up business on a slow night."

I look over at Dudley, who is staring at the TV screen. His mouth hangs open idiotically. In one hand he holds a can of beer; in the other, half of a joint, which has gone out. He is watching a program called *Real Police*. On the TV screen, a row of black teenagers lie face down on the sidewalk with their hands on the backs of their heads. As I watch, the program switches to another shot, in which black teenagers are filing out of a spotlighted doorway, hands on heads, overseen by cops with guns. The cops wear black jackets with glow-in-the-dark lettering on the backs: OPD, DEA, ATF, Sheriff, etc. The teenagers fall face-down on the sidewalk with their hands atop their heads, in a neat row. The cops walk among them, kicking their legs apart, pulling their pockets inside out. A close-up of the palm of a hand, a cop hand, cradling a tiny zip-lock baggie which contains a cocaine rock.

ME: "Look at that kid. He can't be more than eleven." I grope beside the bed for my wine bottle, find it, take a gulp.

DUD: "What?" He looks at me blearily, then takes a deep drag.

ME: "They got kids there. Little kids. Going to jail." I swill some more wine. "I mean . . . look! What's *wrong* with this picture?"

DUD: "What picture?" He squints at the joint, then swallows half a can of beer. It dribbles down his chin. The joint goes out. He re-lights it and takes another toke.

ME: "This program!" I gesture toward the TV with my bottle. "This fucking program! Real Cops! There's an eleven-year-old kid, and that cop is pointing a Real Gun at him! And they're taking him away to Real Jail! And what did he do? He had *one rock!*"

DUD: "What?"

The TV focuses on yet another scene. Black teenagers face down on the sidewalk.

ME: "Look at this one! He had *two* rocks in his pocket! So what? So *kill* them?"

DUD: "Hey. I'm tryna watch TV. These guys broke the Law. It's what they get, smoking that stuff and shit." He waves his beer.

ME: "You used to smoke that shit. Maybe you *still* smoke it, for all I know."

DUD: "Hey, I don't do that shit anymore, OK? I don't wanna talk about it, OK?" He peers at his joint, re-lights it. "They get what they get."

ME: "And look at *this* shit." Wine sloshes as I wave the bottle at the TV screen. More black teenagers face-down in the street. "Might as well be South Africa."

DUD: "Don't start that South Africa shit again. Jesus. You shouldn't drink so much. You shouldn't drink at all, if it's gonna make you crazy."

ME: "But look!"

DUD: "Just shut up. If you don't like the program, don't watch it."

ME: "OK. That's it. I'm leaving." I grab my bag, stuff the bottle in, and leave the room. Slam. I sit in the hall for four hours. There's really no place to go.

Here is a low-class legend:

Arty is a petty drug dealer and a bit of a legend among Those Whose Doors Have Been Kicked In By The Cops.

Arty is sitting in his room, quietly smoking a cocaine rock. The police are banging on the door of his room. He is not responding. He worked hard to get this rock, and he's going to smoke it, and he doesn't care if God Himself is at the door.

"OPD. Open up!" Bangbangbangbangbangbang.

Arty sits smoking his rock. Cops hammer on the door. Cops try various keys to open the door. None of them work. Arty sits, smoking.

"Open the fuck *up!*" The doors are heavy and solid. The cops will have to break it down. They do. The cops wash into the room like a flood. Arty is sitting there smoking his rock. He doesn't acknowledge the presence of anyone else in the room. The cops leap upon Arty and wrestle the pipe from his grasp. They drag him away to jail. Arty says: "Yeah, OK, you got me. But I done smoked my rock!"

. . .

I'm sitting on the bus, by the back door. School kids have swarmed onto the bus, coming home from school. Girls and boys, maybe eleven or twelve years old, mostly black. They fill the bus with their noise and their churning energy.

They take the bus to and from school every day. Some of them have bus passes pinned to their jackets or sweaters. They are churning around in the back of the #57 bus. I notice that some of them are talking about crack. Suddenly they start singing a song about smoking crack:

> "This is the way we smoke a rock
> Smoke a rock
> Smoke a rock
> This is the way
> We smoke a rock . . ."

A children's song.

Arty says: "Crack is the perfect drug for people whose lives are shit, who have never known anything better and have no hope of experiencing anything better. We may have had hope at one time of something better, trying for something better, but what do you do? Do you work harder? Study harder in school? Do we pray to Jesus? What do we do?

"Because none of these things work, and there's really nothing you can do. Your whole life is shit, and always will be. So you smoke a rock, and you don't care. The part of you that cares is totally extinguished. Which is good, because whatever it is you care about is what kills you. You can't afford to care. To care is to open yourself up to more abuse than a person can stand.

"Crack is the perfect drug for people who care about hopeless things. What's the point, anyway? Transported past caring about the hopelessness of your life, the trash heap where you've always lived, your sick and dying family, you are thankful only for the relief. Because you've tried everything you could think of, and even Jesus didn't work. Jesus worked for your grandma, who wore a feed sack dress and carried her Bible five miles to church on Sunday and always made you get down on your knees. She thought Jesus was working, anyway, until she keeled over at the bus stop on the way to church and the ambulance was an hour late, and maybe Jesus didn't work after all. Your parents tried hard work, and worked so hard all their lives, and wound up on welfare anyway. So why bother? You smoke a rock and forget it. Then you die. You gotta die of something, right?"

And then you die.

Imagining a scene which Jessy had described once, where she watched a girl her own age die from crack poisoning in the ER of High Street hospital where she was taking part in a paramedic training class. This teenager had been smoking and smoking and smoking crack, for four or five days straight, and the ER doctors just looked at her and said that there was absolutely nothing they could do, not in a million years did this person have a chance to survive. They'd seen it before, but it affected them because the victim was so young. The students, most of whom were from poor families themselves, had trouble understanding how a human being could get to a place where they would choose death over reality. That sometimes hope is just not enough. Is just not there.

If there truly are two Americas, I was born in the wrong one. The place where I am now, and all the strange and dangerous places I've travelled through to get here, are really only the logical extension of a poverty-stricken childhood and a long line of losers. My whole ancestry is a contradiction, typically American, always plodding onward, unwilling to sink into the swamp which is there waiting for those who stop moving. There is the Native American branch of the family tree, sullen and uncooperative nomads who were harassed and relocated until they disappeared, either killed in battle or, worse, assimilated. Then there was the Scots patriot William Wallace, the bright star on Mom's family tree, who may have been a hero of sorts but was also most certainly a psychotic. Balanced on the other side by my paternal ancestors, the Mennonites, a severe bunch of Bible-toting fundamentalists who were kicked out of every country in Europe for refusing to salute the flag, pay taxes, and serve in the military. These folks doggedly set out in covered wagons looking for a life, and wound up planting themselves directly in the path of the Dust Bowl, the worst agricultural disaster in American history.

And as if this weren't enough, my parents took it upon themselves to become communists and rescue mankind from the greedhead capitalist pigs who had already stolen everything not nailed down, and they ran afoul of Joe McCarthy's HUAC plot in the late 1940s. Barely important enough to be persecuted and certainly not important enough to be prosecuted, we must have been one of the first families in America to go on welfare.

Welfare, as a way of life, leaves much to be desired, although it's probably better than slogging around in covered wagons. If you're born to it there's not really much chance of getting off, ever, especially if you're a woman. While the Real People go through their coming-of-age rituals—the first prom, first date, first car, first kiss, first credit card, driver's license, college, job, engagement, marriage—you are running the gauntlet of the Projects. First cigarette, first drink, first joint, first "sexual encounter," first crime, first arrest, first shot (first intravenous and first subcutaneous "skin-pop" usually count as separate milestones), and by the time you hit the Big One, your First Welfare Check, you're probably in the game forever.

ASHBY: "If I could've gone to a Halloween party this year, I would've gone as a roadkill. I'da painted tire tracks on my face. If there's anything I feel like right now, it's something that's been run over by a hundred cars."
DUDLEY: "You coulda gone to a Halloween party. You're just too lazy. You're too lazy to get out of bed. You're such a parasite."

A lazy rage works its way through Ashby, seething just under the skin. She is almost too tired (or too lazy) to respond to it.
ASHBY: "If I'm a parasite, what does that make *you?* A parasite on a parasite?"
DUDLEY: "I don't want to talk about it."

ASHBY: "I *bet* you 'don't want to talk about it'! You feel guilty about being a parasite on some woman's welfare check? Fucking welfare pimp!"

DUDLEY: "I am not a pimp! I make my own way."

ASHBY: "Sure you make your own way, living off a woman's welfare check. And then go and call *her* a parasite."

DUDLEY: "You want me to beat you up, don't you! You want me to punch your fucking face in . . . you bitch! Don't ever call me a parasite! I work hard for my money! Not my fault that I'm laid off! I didn't ask to get laid off! I work for *my* money. I don't lay around waiting for my check to come in the mail."

ASHBY: "You lay around waiting for *my* check to come in the mail. You fraud! You're kidding yourself—you're not kidding *me*. I've been a parasite on the system since I was fucking born! And I say Fuck the system! And Fuck You!"

Later, in bed, Ashby says "Could you just hold me, or hug me a little?"

DUDLEY: (Still angry) "No way! Well, maybe." He gives her a little squeeze. "OK?"

ASHBY: "Can I hold *you?* I just want to hold something, go to sleep holding something. . . ."

DUDLEY: "I get real uncomfortable with somebody, like, touching me. I can't sleep, if somebody is *touching* me."

They have had this argument many times.

ASHBY: "You got a horrible problem. You don't want to fuck, and you don't want anybody *touching* you, even if the room is *freezing* we can't have any human warmth, not even a warm bod in the bed, for god's sake. I have to sleep in the same bed with a stiff, for god's sake!"

DUDLEY: "Well, we only got one bed, so we both have to sleep in it together unless you want to sleep on the floor. But none of this cuddling and touching shit, OK?"

Ashby stares at the ceiling, seething, grinding her teeth.

ASHBY: "Stiff! Why should *I* sleep on the floor? Why don't *you* sleep on the floor? Or we could take *turns*. But no. . . ."

Of course, Dudley has fallen asleep. He snores horribly. He even sleeps like a stiff, at attention, often maintaining the same position all night. Ashby wants to kick him out of bed with both feet, just Blam! Make him bounce off the wall. He'll lie there on the floor blinking, uncomprehending, while she jumps up and down on his moronic countenance, stomps him into the rug, then dumps the mangled body out the window. Who would notice, who would care? Then she'd go live in the mountains, drink clean water, listen to the birdies sing. Happily ever after. Listen to trees rustle in the wind, by the creek, listen to the water slide over the rocks. Happily. Ever. After.

I am riding on the 57 bus, a few days after Halloween, watching an old half-passed-out nodding drunk and waiting for him to fall off his seat. Suddenly he wakes up, snaps to attention, and looks around with an expression of wonderment. "Oh, man!" he says. "I done been born into the wrong world!"

12.

Saint Vinnie's

Ashby sits on a bench in the little plaza on fourteenth and Broadway, near the public library kiosk, fishing cracker crumbs from the bottom of her bag to throw at the pigeons. At the other end of the bench an old wino slumps, apparently dozing. Office workers, businesspeople, and an occassional tourist hurry past.

"They get off on us, you know," Ashby says to the wino, indicating the 'normal' people. "Most of them probably don't even know it. But they do. They feed on us. They see us in the shit, and think *they're* not. Ha." She looks up at the APL building. "That's the *real* shit, if you ask me. At least I can get up and walk away from this shit. And go on to other shit. Maybe it won't be better shit, but it'll be *different* shit."

"Mmuh," says the wino.

"And at least I *know* it's shit. They're all wondering why their lives aren't quite like what they see on TV, probably. And their lives don't quite measure up to TV, so they think there's something horribly wrong with them. But then they look at us and they feel better. They *need* us. We sustain their illusions about themselves."

"Thas' it," says the wino.

"But it's not enough," Ashby goes on, inspired by her own speech. "That's why they're always making things worse for us, and why there are more and more of us all the time. Because how many of those normal, ordinary, everyday people are getting evicted right now at this moment, getting laid off, getting their houses and cars repo'ed, getting tossed into the shit? And how long does it take the average newcomer to figure out that nobody feels sorry for them? About two weeks?"

"Humma nun," says the wino.

"And then they start screaming 'Hey! Look at poor me, here in the shit! You're supposed to feel sorry for me!' And the Man says 'Oh, but we *do!*' And the person screams 'Then why don't you *help* me?' And the Man says 'Oh, but we *are!*' And so the poor fucker gets all confused. And most likely stays that way."

"I worked thirty-sevum year for the railroad," says the wino. "I done. Thirty-seven. Yeah, uh."

"Congratulations," says Ashby.

I find myself thinking about food all the time, as though I were starving, but actually I am overweight. I notice that a lot of the people who eat regularly at the Free Dining Room are fat, but not healthily so. They seem bloated, like bread that is rising, as though if you poked your finger into their flesh the indentation would stay there. But this is too paranoid, even for me. I know the symptoms of malnutrition and am projecting. . . .

I get so terribly hungry standing in line at the Dining Room, but then when the food is in front of me the hunger vanishes and I feel nauseated. I watch other women scraping food into jars and bags they have brought. This is not against the rules. We are allowed to take food to a friend or family member who isn't able to make it to the Dining Room, for a child. . . .

An unkempt hispanic woman stuffs macaroni and cheese into a large jar and shoves it into her bag. The woman is grossly fat, lethargic and stupid-looking. Her eyes are dull and blank, as though there were no brain behind them. But you can tell that she is not taking food to

71

bring to someone else, she is taking it for herself, for later. For when she gets so hungry that she can't stand it.

When people get hungry enough they'll eat grass, trees, mud. But this is not a deprived skeleton, barren of flesh. This woman looks as though she could live off her fat for months. Yet she looks almost dead. Dead of what?

Oakland will not have masses of starving skeletons wandering the streets with bony hands outstretched, vertebrae and ribs and pelvic bones poking through the skin. No Nazi death camps here, folks. Oakland will have huge, sluggish, masses of bloated fat people with dead eyes. Dying of starvation as we get fatter. Groping with bloated sausage fingers for something, anything, rat poison, we'll cram it in. Because they aren't killing us, they're feeding us. How can we complain?

Dudley and I walk down to St. Vinnie's Free Dining Room for the Thanksgiving dinner. Today we are accompanied by Bob, a friend of Dudley's from the Dregs Hotel on Fourteenth Street, who works as a night security guard somewhere downtown. He makes minimum wage, and after he pays his rent at the Dregs he doesn't have much left for food. He is a small, waiflike kid with a fading black eye from a beating he received on the job from a gang of strangers.

Bob tells us, "I was just doing my rounds and they jumped me. They weren't trying to break in or anything, just looking for somebody to beat up. I was there, so they beat me up. They fucking knocked me out. I came to and they were gone. They stole my wallet and my flashlight."

I ask him if he's been to a doctor. He says no—Ruff'n'Reddy Security don't pay for that. I ask him if he quit.

"Who can afford to quit? I'm lucky to have this job."

"Wrong kind of luck, Bob," I tell him.

We walk in silence down San Pablo Avenue. Across the street I see the legless black man in the wheelchair who lives in one of the San Pablo hotels. The guy is surrounded by his buddies as usual, laughing loudly, telling jokes. He has a big boombox attached to his wheelchair, between the wheels, always playing loud soul music. I wonder how the guy maintains his amazing good humor. Of course, he probably drinks a lot, but does that account for it? A lot of people get depressed when they drink, and what could be more depressing than to be a legless guy in a wheelchair, probably a Vietnam vet, living in a scummy hotel on San Pablo by the scummy bus station? What's this guy's secret, and how come he's not out committing suicide somewhere?

At St. Vinnie's we split up. There are different lines for men and women, and the men's line is at least ten times longer. It seems that family values have struck out here, too, and the sexes must be separated even on a holiday. Women, almost all of them black, are standing in line on the opposite side of the courtyard. Many are holding babies; some have three or four kids. There are pregnant women and old women. They rarely have to stand in line for more than ten minutes. The men have to wait at least an hour.

Inside the doorway I pick up my tray and plasticware. There is an armed guard standing in the doorway. Behind the serving counter is a line of volunteers, the Nice Old Ladies. They pass my plate from one to the next, dishing food into it. The traditional Thanksgiving grub: turkey slices in gravy, mashed potatoes, yams, greens, bread. The scene is overseen by a smiling old nun with gray hair under a small cap-and-veil, a knee-length gray uniform, and a wise face. This nun, you can tell, has seen it all: murder, mayhem, physical violence, dead babies, child abuse, bloodshed, you name it. Yet she remains cheery, full of smiles, her face flushed with goodwill. She is like the wheelchair guy, unshakable in her belief in the goodness of god or man or both.

I sit down with my tray containing the plate of food, the drink (powdered milk or juice) and a slice of home-baked American apple pie.

On each table are large jars with holes punched in the lids, full of salt and pepper. (When I return the following week there is a sign on the door, hand-lettered on cardboard: OUR SALT AND PEPPER JARS HAVE BEEN STOLEN. THEY WILL NOT BE REPLACED!)

I look down at the plate of food, suddenly not hungry. I'll ask the nun for a piece of foil, so I can take my dinner home. I pick at the pie crust with my plastic fork.

"Some meal, huh," says the woman next to me, a sad-faced droopy woman of indeterminate age.

"Every time I eat here I get sick," I tell her.

"Yeah," the woman agrees. "They poison it. The food."

"You think so?" I ask, rhetorically.

"They poison the homeless," she says, stuffing turkey into her mouth. "They want to kill us. They do it slow."

"*Nuns* put poison in the food?" I ask, trying not to sound surprised. Or to sound as though I disbelieve the woman, who may at any moment whip out a huge knife and try to slit my throat for calling her a liar.

But the sad woman just droops further down, chewing with loose teeth. "Yeah. They does."

"But . . ." wanting to know more, trying to sound indifferent, "they're *nuns*. They're religious. Nuns wouldn't do stuff like that."

The woman glances at me sideways, fork poised "You Cathlik?"

"Uh . . . no. . . ."

"Then you don't know *nothin'* about nuns."

End conversation. It is dangerous to try to talk to people at the Dining Room, even on holidays. I wrap my pie in the foil, dump the rest of the dinner in the trash. The nun smiles at me. Brides of the dumb bleeding Christ.

A St. Vinnie's Fantasy

Two hungry, homeless Jews go to St. Vinnie's on Passover. They stand in line, eyeing the food. Rolls! Buns! Donuts! Baloney! Salami! Maca-roni'n'Cheese!

JEW #1: (to buddy) "Can we eat macaroni and cheese?"

JEW #2: "I dunno. I don't think so. Better pass on that."

JEW #1 (to Nice Old Lady volunteer): "What else ya got?"

N.O.L.: "Spinach with bacon grease."

JEW #2: "Oy vey."

And so on.

St. Vinnie's!

13.

Locked Out

I got locked out of the hotel again last night, this time through no fault of my own. When I went out, to do some shopping and laundry, there was some sort of hubbub taking place in the hotel entryway: a Patel was trying to evict the Blonde Whore from the lobby while the Desk Guy rounded up The Doomed and sent them shuffling off to their rooms. The Blonde Whore cussing loudly and imaginatively, trashing the Patel along with many of his relatives and ancestors, her troupe divided along lines of support. I could see that many of them had turned against her in defense of the Patel, doubtless in fear of their possible placement on the Hotel Shit List.

When I returned to the hotel with my bag of laundry and an additional bag of groceries, the front door was solidly locked. Four or five tenants were standing dejectedly in the entryway, including the Droopy Woman, who was sniffling and crying. The Desk Guy could be seen dimly behind the desk, hiding behind a fully opened National Inquisitor.

"He's not letting nobody in," I was told. "They was a fight. He's heavily pissed."

"The owners told him not to," says another voice, defending the

Desk Guy. "It's his job."

Fuck this. I walk the three blocks to the BART Plaza with my bags getting heavier and heavier. It's cold and dark, and I wasn't wearing my jacket when I left the hotel. I decide to call Adeline.

"You just come right on over here," Adeline tells me on the phone. "I always have room for you, my dear."

Adeline lives in a shared house in Richmond. It takes me over an hour to get there on the bus. It's the first time I've been there since I helped Adeline move in. The lights are all blazing in the house; the rest of the block is dark and quiet. A jowly scowling lumberjack dyke answers the door, looking me up and down with intense disapproval.

"I come to visit Adeline," I say, certain that she won't let me in and I'll have to climb the fence and bang on Adeline's window. But she silently steps aside for me to pass with plenty of room, as though I were contagious.

Adeline has had a new lock put on her bedroom door, which she carefully locks behind me, along with the sliding bolt and the hook-and-eye. She goes into her little bathroom and returns with two clean glasses. In twenty-five years of visiting, I've never shown up without a bottle of wine. She opens the wine while I unpack groceries: cheese, bread, lunch meat, sardines, potato chips, and dip. When Dudley and I buy groceries to eat in our room, this is what we usually get. Leftovers are wrapped carefully in many layers to prevent cockroach invasion.

"Food!" Adeline retrieves plates and a kitchen knife from her bathroom. "Bitches won't let a person *in* the kitchen around here," she says, nodding to indicate the rest of the house. "Bitches eat your food, steal anything that ain't locked up." Adeline does not get along with her housemates, who don't get along with each other. "Good thing I got my own toilet, or I'd be pissing out the window."

The TV is turned up loud, blasting out a car commercial. Adeline adjusts the sound with her remote.

"So it's not getting any better in the house." I can't think of anything better to say at the moment.

"Ha." Bitterly. "Bitches thought they'd get points for letting a nigger move in with them. Right." She has made a sandwich, and takes a bite. "Racist bitches. Get a nigger in the house, automatically assume it's free maid service. Dirty clothes and dirty dishes everywhere. I do not touch anything which does not belong to me."

"Can I sleep on your floor tonight? The hotel locked me out."

"Mi casa su casa, my dear. Are the Patels being mean to you again?"

"Making my life a living hell." I pour more wine. "If only I could find a nice house like this."

"Ah yes. Too-shay. We'll probably all be evicted soon anyway." Adeline aims her remote at the TV, turns the volume way up. "'*Must* you have your *television* on *all* the time, dear?'"she mimics."'It just *simply* rots your brain out.' Your brain, my asshole! I need to discover *more* stuff I can do that they 'just absolutely hate.' White trash racist bitches."

Of course, the fact that Adeline is chronically paranoid and notoriously hard to get along with doesn't mean that her housemates are *not* absolute bitches and racist to boot. I've spent a lot of time trying to figure out what turns her wheels, how it must feel to be a black woman in America. I've decided that there's not much that's worse than being a black woman in America today, and that Adeline's attitude is defensible if not altogether rational.

"Oh, don't mind *me,* dear." It has suddenly occurred to Adeline that I myself am white trash. "I'm just in a evil mood. I needed this hooch" she pours more wine in my glass "which you so thoughtfully provided."

I reach for a cigarette. "Aren't we *all* racist bitches."

"I wouldn't call someone who hates *everybody* a racist, my dear." She raises her glass, to me.

"I couldn't put up with this kind of share-housey shit for a second," I declare. "Better the Patels."

"Only time I get treated like white folks is when I put on a sari," Adeline tells me. "But I will never go to the Patels. Never. I'd go back to my husband before I'd go to the Patels. Shit."

I lie down on the rug, wrapped in the quilt Adeline has thrown me, using my bag of laundry for a pillow. The TV blasts surrealistically. "I need some good drugs," I groan.

"Drink to that," Adeline raises her glass.

Journal Entry: I've been sitting in the dark, being sad. Of course, I had to turn on the light to write, but it's not much better. This morning I woke up in knots again, a sort of convulsion in slow motion. If I could just loosen up a little in my sleep. I can control the tension somewhat if I'm awake, but in sleep I just go into knots and wake up rigid, my back and neck stiff, a kind of rigor mortis you get while you're still alive.

This goes with dreams of being crushed under unbearable burdens or forced into impossibly small spaces; being squeezed, being forced, being crushed. The emotion is hate and rage, horrible anger and fury and rage, but not fear. No fear, just an uncontrollable anger at being squeezed into some place where it's impossible for you to go.

I want to have good dreams but I can't. I try, and wake up in knots again. My body wakes up in tangled knots of emotional fury, and I am sorry and sad. I am too fragmented to even apologize to myself. The infuriated can't forgive the apologist. The same old war, same old shit.

But I still desperately want my dreams back. I used to look forward to sleep because even if the waking world was unbearable I'd have happy and satisfying dreams. Maybe I didn't hate myself so much then. Now my dreams have turned against me. How can your own *dreams* turn against you? Dreams are supposed to be sacred. When everything else turns to shit, the sentimentalists say, you still have your dreams.

If these dreams are mine, then I really have nothing left. Except maybe the absence of fear. I fight in my dreams, I punch and kick people, push them in front of trucks, yell and scream and cuss them out. Maybe that's something. At least I'm not afraid.

Dream State

The prevailing image is of . . . being in a very small room with dirty walls, a bare lightbulb hanging from the ceiling. Cobwebs. Either there is no window, or the window is painted over, nailed shut. Can't tell if it's day or night, dawn or twilight. Twilight falling . . . stop. You can't write poetry in the midst of this shit. Unless you have . . . good drugs?

The idea of the good old days, so long ago. Maybe they weren't so good, what with living in abandoned buildings and all, nothing to eat but beans at Cheap Tony's. No poetry, dirty walls, mattress on the floor. Sleeping bag rolled up, backpack for a pillow. No possibility of food. Just drugs. With drugs, the dirty walls and bare bulb and filthy mattress don't matter. Everything opens up into infinite possibilities. The dirty walls open up. The bare bulb is a sun, shining benevolently on a universe of possibilities.

14. My Script My Movie,

Sometimes I feel like I'm outside myself watching my own movie about myself. This movie is always playing inside my head somewhere, and sometimes when I have nothing else to do I check the schedule to find out where it's playing in my head or maybe I walk in on it by accident, or maybe I get a message that somebody has to do something about the goddamned movie right now and of course I'm stuck with the job because it's my movie, isn't it?

So I look around and check out the audience, which is always the same: a couple of bored and cynical old dope-smoking intellectuals sitting in the back who will remember everything you say and criticize it forever, and I have to narrate the movie to them, always putting in a few little gems for them to save for playback later and maybe get a cynical smile for a second or two, but I'll never get to see it because they never have expressions on their faces when I'm around.

And then there's the horrible jerk loudly eating something in the middle of the first row, right in front of the screen always, and he's regressed back past kindergarten into day care but I have to narrate the movie in such a way that he'll understand, too, though I never know whether he's listening or not, and he probably isn't and never has and never will, but it doesn't matter.

Sometimes I just have to crack the door a little and peek at the movie to see which reel is playing and then I can go do something else, or go back to doing nothing at all.

"You buy, I fly," says Dudley. Which means: If you buy me a six-pack, I'll run out to the store.

I put down my journal and reach for my bag, where I know I've stashed a ten-dollar bill. I find it, hand it to him. He flies.

Dudley rarely asks about my writing and seems genuinely uninterested in it, which I take as a stroke of incredible good luck. He is not jealous of it, which means few interruptions from him. And most people who come across a writer at work seem to be compelled to interrupt, feel it is their *duty* to interrupt, that they are doing you a big *favor* by interrupting your work. Or can it even be called *work?* Perhaps the writer is subconsciously asking, *begging,* to be relieved of the burden. The curse. The obsession, the compulsion to get it out, write it down, give the word-demon a life of its own so you can go on with yours, such as it is.

Writer at Work, a fable

You are chewing the pencil or pounding the machine, caught in your obsession to write something out. Somebody comes into the room.

UG (for Uninvited Guest): "Hey! You'll never guess what I just saw! Guess what I just fucking *saw!*"

WRITER (sighing patiently): "OK. What did you just see?"

UG: "Well, I was walking down the street, right?"

WRITER: "Right."

UG: "And there was this *guy* walking down the street. And he was coming from the corner store, 'cause he had a six-pack in a bag. You know how you can always tell when there's a six-pack in the bag, right? Like, it has this certain *shape,* right? So you can tell this guy just got off of work, and he stopped at the store to buy a six-pack, like usual, you know, like he does every day when he gets off work?"

WRITER: "Right."

UG: "And he's got this *dog* with him on a leash, right? He's walking the *dog* while he goes for the beer, right? And the dog starts barking, right? So this guy is walking down the street with his six-pack and his fucking *dog* on the leash, and it starts barking, right?"

WRITER (sighing impatiently): "So what happened?"

UG: "*That's* what happened! I mean, it was *too* bizarre!"

WRITER: "And *then* what?"

UG: "Whaddaya mean *then what?* I'm just telling you what *happened,* okay? I mean, I had this experience and you don't even *care!*"

WRITER: "Some guy with beer and a dog, big deal."

UG: "You *see!* You just don't *care* about anything except your stupid *writing!* You're so wrapped *up* in yourself! It's not healthy! Something's *wrong* with you. The whole *world* could come to an end and you'd just sit there with your stupid *writing.* You're all fucked up!"

WRITER: "Get out! Go fuck yourself!"

Moral: Don't waste your time trying to be polite.

Dudley probably regards writing as just another symptom of my psychosis, which of course it may be, and which is fine with me.

My current journal is small, the size of a modest hardcover book, with blank, unlined pages. I write in pen, sometimes fine-lined and conservatively cramped, sometimes in sprawling scrawls with headlines and footnotes and things pasted in and sketches in different colors. I try to let my different voices say whatever they want.

I would rather type. I have spent so much time sitting at the typewriter that I feel totally at home there. I had a big old Selectric at school and wish I could have one here. But it would make noise, and blow fuses if I could find a place to plug it in, which there isn't, and would probably get stolen by junkies if left alone in the room. Someday, the Children tell me, I will have a word processor and rule my own world.

Journal Entry: I went to the chiropractor today. She told me she was very pleased at how much I've improved in the past few months, how much I've loosened up. This worries me. It means that my repressed fears and angers are losing their grip. Which would be a dream come true if I were in a stable situation, but the way things are now it seems dangerous. I keep getting powerful urges to scream and throw things and break windows, to let it all out. But I hang on. I wonder what They'd do to me *now?* Probably turn me into one of the doomed. *Maybe I'd like it.* That's what scares me. I think I really could kill myself at this point. Goodbye and good riddance.

The avoid-reality-at-all-costs, jump-from-the-train state of mind. The rat zigzags frantically across the shattered grey landscape, looking for a hole. . . .

> The frazzled rat of my mind, skittering around inside my skull. Looking for a way out?
> Feels like my head's full of ashes.
> Wheels warped and askew.
> The rat. The rat. The sorry rat.
> Jump.

When my own head seems an unacceptable place to live and I can't squeeze a word out on the page, I pick up a book and get into someone else's head. Someone else is there to take me away somewhere; that's why they published this book. To fulfill a need. Do you need to be taken away from yourself for your own protection? Read this book, watch this movie. Watch TV if you can stand it—my dreams are usually better than TV, but it does serve the purpose of putting me to sleep.

I write down a lot of my dreams, but I wouldn't put most of them in a book. Nothing is more boring than reading about other people's dreams. Still, if nobody ever tried to express their dreams, we wouldn't have fiction. If nobody ever just let themselves *go* into some ridiculous fantasy we wouldn't have Oz, or Alice, or Xanadu.

Great lines sometimes pop into my head and are instantly forgotten because my first thought is "*That's* not mine, it's too good. I must have heard it somewhere or read it somewhere." I've probably lost a hundred times more stuff than I've ever written down. But who knows, maybe they do all come back around sometime. If I thought of it once, it'll probably surface again, hopefully when I have a good place to put it.

15. The Rap

The weekly Womens' Rap is an event I attend sometimes. I don't really enjoy it, and sometimes I hate it, but I go anyway. It's free. The theme is demoralization. It's supposed to be therapy. They say it helps to sit around yapping about your problems. Maybe it does. Nobody really knows.

I go mainly to listen to the stories. Amazing how you hear the same stories from different people. And one is permitted to talk about any goddamned thing, even clothes.

mary ellen:
"The worst thing was that I stank. In the middle of winter when the pipes were frozen and Ma didn't have money for the laundromat, and all I had was this horrible jacket that my Ma found somewhere, and it had something in it like cat piss, you know, something that you can never get rid of the smell. It made *me* sick, the smell, but it was all I had and it was cold back there, I mean freezing.

"My Ma and Pa grew up on dirt farms, where *everything* stank, so maybe they never noticed, or they thought it shouldn't bother anybody, a little thing like that. So it was just *my* particular problem, my own personal little gripe, having to go to school and be the only kid that smelled like a barnyard. Maybe the smell of that jacket reminded them of home. A nice homey smell, you know? Kinda reminds ya of the good ol' days, don't it? Good ole Oklahomee sheepshit aroma.

"So I got sick of my friends avoiding me, and my friends' parents cringing away. So I gave up having friends. You'd think I'd have had the sense just to get rid of the fucking jacket, right? Well, in my family you didn't do things like that. My Ma would be screaming and crying and keeling over with a heart attack. 'You lost your *jacket?* Oh my God! My God! Whatever will we *do!*'

"So I wore the fucking thing all winter. And then they ask me why don't I have any friends any more? And I say 'Fuck you! Go on and send your kid to school stinking like the City Dump and then ask why the kid has no friends and stays in the corner looking out the window. Maybe it's OK for a *boy* to go around smelling like a dead skunk but not, for god's sake, if there even *is* a god, a *girl!* Not in Detroit! Not in the City of Detroit!' Which, just as of itself, smells bad enough.

"I mean, I'd tried so hard to be accepted, putting little barrettes in my hair and shit, pinning my clothes up so they wouldn't look like I was wearing somebody else's clothes, which never fooled anybody. I mean, the more I tried, the more pitiful I looked. Pitiful and stinking.

"That's the reason I came to California and stayed here. Because here you can just wear a sweater or two in the winter. I don't want to ever look at another jacket in my life."

jackie:

"When I was pregnant with the second kid, he started bringing his other girlfriends to the apartment. He brought this girl Bingo. He says 'Bingo has to go to court in the morning, and she got nothing to wear,' and he asked me to loan her my best dress, my only good dress, you know, and I did, because I knew he'd take it anyway if I said no.

"And of course I never got it back, and he says 'she told me she'd give it back and she didn't. Not my fault.'" Jackie snorts into a wad of kleenex she's been wringing in her hands. "Then he brings *two* girls, and he says 'they just got in town, and they got nothing to wear,' and he gives them more of my stuff. And I never got *that* back. And finally I got no clothes left except this dress I made outta a bedspread. And the only reason he don't give *that* away is 'cause it looks so raggedy.

"So finally I'm so mad I don't care if he hits me. I say 'I'm gonna find those chicks and beat them up and get my fuckin' clothes back.' And he says 'You better not even *think* about doing that, cause I'll *kill* you.'

"And here I am nine months pregnant, with the first kid still in diapers, and he says 'I fix it so you can't even leave the *house,* bitch.'" Jackie sighs deeply, mopping up tears. "He never got me anything for my birthday. He never had the bread for that. But he felt guilty about it, so he'd beat me up. He'd stay out extra late and get extra drunk and come home where I was asleep and drag me outa the bed and beat my ass. I was always hoping he'd forget my birthday, but he never did. An extra black eye, is what I got. Some birthday present."

carolyn (who always shows up but rarely makes sense):
"I lost it. Somewhere. More trees will grow somewhere maybe, but they cut mine down and tore the roots out. Now they've built a wall between me and some way to survive which nobody can see but me. Sometimes I'm working all morning all afternoon all evening and it's not work because you didn't make any money. It's only work if you get paid for it. If you get paid. Get the kids up feed them dress them get them off to school go to school go to class come home clean up wash dishes take wash to the laundromat buy food at the store cook it feed the kids clean up wash the dishes do your homework do their homework put them to bed and you didn't do any work because you didn't get paid. So therefore, you have done nothing. Lazy bitch.

"They say we don't deserve to live."

Finally, they get tired of me just sitting there and listening, and they begin to suspect that I am just another sociology major in sheep's clothing, and they ask me to tell my story.

So I tell them a story from my own miserable and depressing past, one of the more innocuous ones:

ME: "I didn't leave him, because I had no place to go. I should have left him. I just couldn't. He was crazy. He'd take speed and stay up for days. One time we were in a car with a bunch of people driving up from L.A. And he was freaking out that there were choppers following us in the air, and they were coming down from outer space to zero in on him. And I said no, I was trying to reassure him, you know, they're not from outer space, it's just the Channel Five chopper with the traffic report.

"And then he just looked at me and said 'You're one of *Them*.'

"And I said no, there is no *Them*, it's just the Channel Five Eye In The Sky traffic check, you know?

"And he said 'You are an alien from outer space and you're one of Them. *I* know.'

"And I said no, and he said 'don't lie to me. Don't *ever* lie to me' . . . and then he hit me on the top of my head as hard as he could, blam! And he was a big strong guy. Right on the top of my head. I saw stars, and I was out for I don't know how long, thinking Wow! You really *do* see stars! And when I came to, the other people in the car were saying to him: Why did you *do* that? Why did you *do* that to her? And I'm saying: Why did you *do* that to me? Why do you have to *do* these things to me? You're supposed to love me and take care of me! And he's saying Fuck you, you don't know what you're talking about.

"And a week later I woke up in the morning with *two* black eyes, from getting hit like that on the top of my head. And I had two black eyes for a month. And I actually *looked* like an alien from outer space, then. I looked like a refugee from *Star Trek*. It took me a long time to get over it, and all that time I was thinking: It serves you right!"

The Stiff

The back of my neck feels hot and tight. At the base of the skull, from the excruciating point where the spine begins, around behind and below the earlobes, to the hinges of the jawbone. When I remember to think about the jawbone, I discover it clenched as in *rigor mortis*. Premature *rigor mortis*. When I open my mouth wide the hinges of the jaw snap and pop. My jaw has probably been clenched for hours, and I can't even remember how long. I have trouble talking. Keep Your Mouth Shut is the rule. If They ask you something, nod. Or shake your head. Yes or no. Always better to say no. Best to not even say it, just shake the head. Or don't do anything. When I shake my head the cervical vertebrae crack and pop. A stiff. I am a stiff.

Hold your head up! Keep your mouth shut! If you look at Them They'll think you're guilty! If you don't look at Them They'll think you're guilty! Put your shoulders back! If you have breasts, hunch your shoulders forward! Pull in your gut! Sit up straight! Don't wiggle your hips! Protect the vulnerable midriff! Keep your feet pointed straight ahead! Put one foot exactly in front of the other when you walk! Keep your spine straight! Keep your knees stiff! Keep your elbows at your sides! Don't wiggle your shoulders! Keep your eyes down! Keep your chin up! Don't turn your head! Don't look out of the corners of your eyes! Don't smile! Don't frown! Don't wrinkle your brow! Don't laugh! Don't cry! Keep your fucking mouth shut!

Now you have a stiff walking around, and nobody wants a stiff. You have allowed Them to do this to you. You are what They made you, but you are not what They want. They always blame the victim.

This is my body, but it is not mine. It is what They made it. They told me how to make it behave. But there were too many contradictions. All I have now is a faulty machine. Every night I wake up in knots, contradicted. I have this body, this head, this heart, all they do is contradict each other. Even in sleep. Why bother even trying to sleep?

I don't want this body.

16. Food Fight at St. Vinnie's

The bag lady examines her tray of food (hunger pangs vs. abdominal cramps) in the St. Vinnie's Free Dining Room. Grim food. Food for the Grim. Eat now, suffer later.

Suddenly a high-pitched "Yelp!" is heard from the mens' side, followed by a deep voice booming "Gaw-Damn!"

The heads of the women and children come up, on instant alert, like a herd of startled moose. Through a gap in the partition the bag lady sees a black man slowly rise, canned peach slices sliding off of his bald head.

The peached man scoops up a handful of macaroni and cheese, fashions it into a sloppy ball, and lobs it into the face of a white guy at the next table. The guy struggles to his feet, sending a horrible greasy glob of lentils into his neighbor's lap. The neighbor then leaps up and, swinging his tray like a giant fly-swatter, swats the white guy onto the table behind them. A geyser of Kool-Aid erupts into the air. Across the room, a skinny demented dude jumps onto a table and screams "Food Fiiight!" Day-old donuts slice through the air like shrapnel.

On the women's side a young woman grabs her children and

disappears out the women's entranceway. A decrepit old hag begins to cackle loudly and hysterically. A permanently-pissed-off black woman heaves a pitcher of watered-down powdered milk over the partition into the men's area, yelling "Mothafuckas! Mothafuckas!"

The Nice Old Ladies behind the serving counter glance around in confusion, adjusting hearing aids and glasses. The woman who had been sitting next to the departed mother and children begins to toss their almost-full trays over the partition.

The security guard, who has been standing frozen in astonishment between the men's and women's areas suddenly unfreezes, reaches for his gun and opens his mouth to issue a command. Before he can get the gun out he is engulfed in an avalanche of tepid macaroni and wilted lettuce, his mighty voice reduced to a bubbling "Urg."

Several women jump up and rush to rescue their men. Several men come flying into the women's area to rescue their women. The partitions go down, one falling onto a table of women and the other onto a table of men. The Nice Old Ladies fall to the floor behind the counter in reasonable imitation of bartenders in an old western movie shoot-out.

A crazed-looking woman has reached behind the counter and dragged out a huge metal tray of cold slimy macaroni which she tosses into the air, a handful at a time, rice at an unspeakable wedding.

Like a wet dog, the guard is shaking himself loose from the foul grip of the food. He takes one step and falls on his ass. A river of lentil soup is creeping down the main aisle. More people go down. They crawl around on hands and knees coated with rancid bacon grease, unable to regain footing. There is a sudden cloudburst of plastic spoons and forks. A legless Vietnam Vet is pounding out a rhythm on his wheelchair with an empty gallon can, chanting "Ho, Ho, Ho Chi Minh!" Trays sail through the air like frisbees.

The bag lady gets up and makes her way to the exit, stepping carefully over puddles of congealing substances. Outside in the sunshine a kindly-looking old wino is blissfully scattering breadcrumbs into a shuffle of tattered pigeons. Sirens can be heard in the distance.

17. The Bag Lady Reads *Hamlet* by the Shores of Lake Merritt

You'd put on something like one of those big, waterproof down jackets, maybe. This might actually help keep you afloat until it started absorbing water. You could pin the flowers to it, or stick them down in around your neck. Not nettles, though. You couldn't get very far with nettles around your neck.

But should the note be *mad?* Or quotes. That's it, apt quotes. Or a real note. She didn't leave a note, of course. But you'd have to leave a note. Xerox the note, in case something happened to the first one, or it didn't get found, or that crazy old guy smoked it before somebody found it.

"I left a note," the Baglady announces to the Imaginary Press, "But this old guy smoked it. He smoked my suicide note!!" How's that for an original Lake Merritt legend?

You could just write "Adios, motherfuckers," on the note. But leave the skull there, right? Put the skull on top of the note, like a paperweight. But then nobody would be able to raise any doubts as to the death not being deliberate. And it's always fun to see some asshole pop up (light-bulb goes on over his head) and say "But—but maybe it was an accident!"

"Right!" Hoots of derisive laughter from the Feminist Community. "Like Juliet just slipped and fell on the knife while she was cleaning it."

"She din' know it wuz loaded, har har."

So anyway, you swim out toward the middle, and hope you can get close to the middle before you sink. Only for the sake of artistry and symmetry, of course. And hope the fucker is *deep* enough. Embarrassing if the son of a bitch only came up to your shoulders, and you're standing in there like an idiot.

But now comes the brilliant part. You always have to take into account that maybe nobody will notice, right? And also the possibility that they'll notice but they won't *care*. But you don't want to be flailing around yelling out there and maybe give some idiot time to rescue you. So listen to this part:

You've got your flowers. A lot of daisies, because they're bright and will show up against the water. Also, they grow everywhere, so they're always available, and they're free. And you maybe get a couple of those purple orchids, like they wear to the high school prom. They cost, but hey. *You* won't be needing your money anymore. So take what's left of your welfare check and go down to the flower stand.

Then, you anchor your flowers to little flotation devices, pieces of styrofoam, or balloons with just a little air. And tied loosely together so they'll spread out but not scatter. And hanging below, a little weight, so they won't blow down the storm drain if it's windy. And there's your perfect scenario.

Scenario:

Mad Ophelia is out in the middle of Lake Merritt. Her clothes fill with water and she sinks. On the surface, a scattering of flowers floating! And on the bank, by the willow tree, a note written in the lady's delicate hand, weighed down by a skull!

Next day, in the Oakland press:

An unidentified woman reportedly drowned in Lake Merritt yesterday. Police divers are still searching for the body.

In an unrelated incident, a pair of lunchtime joggers discovered a human skull yesterday by the Lake Merritt jogging path. Authorities are trying to ascertain the identity of the skull through dental records. County Coroner's Office spokesperson Winifred Blatt told the press, "We speculate that [the skull] was left in the park by a Voodoo cult, whose members often use such objects in their rituals." As of this reporting, there has been no further comment from the Coroner's Office.

Lake Merritt sulks in the sun, refusing to give up its dead. Of which there must be a substantial number, as the lake and the surrounding park possess the aspect of a natural oubliette into which the discards and detritus of the surrounding society are inevitably drawn. The kind of urban sinkhole you'll find in every city. Sometimes, especially on cloudy days, the lake takes on an evil aura, the sort of dead-end entropic evil which is static, stagnant, and dull, and has an average depth of about three feet.

The Baglady has finished feeding the seagulls, and is feeding the squirrels. She does this often, as it gives her immense pleasure to provide sustenance to creatures more helpless and dependent than herself. Most of the squirrels in this area are quite tame, and she enjoys watching them remove the shell from a peanut, turning the nut in their tiny hands, end over end, until the kernel becomes accessible.

She sits on the grass not far from the water's edge, her bag beside her along with a half-empty can of beer, a dog-eared paperback book, and the remains of a bag lunch from the Free Lunch Church, most of which has been tossed to the seagulls. At the top of the gentle slope behind her and to the right, three homeless black men sit under a tree passing around a two-liter plastic bottle of Frisco. In the other direction a fiendish little old man sits smoking a newspaper, rolling the sheets up one by one, lighting them, chuckling to himself and puffing away in a cloud of horrible smoke.

The Baglady thinks this is extraordinarily funny. The little guy's clothes are in complete tatters, he has wisps and spikes of white hair sticking out from his head in all directions, and he appears to have no teeth. He has the appearance of a sort of comical demon, who might at any instant vanish in a cloud of his own smoke. She wonders if he's picky about which periodical he prefers; the *Chronicle* over the *Trib*, perhaps. Or the *Wall Street Journal*. Maybe he will smoke only the *Wall Street Journal*, and if one is not available in the East Bay will go all the way to the Pacific Stock Exchange in San Francisco to go through the trash there.

Joggers plod endlessly around the lake, rats in a wheel. The whole place might as well be in a toxic coma. Poisoned molecules whirling frantically in the death dance. Oaks used to grow freely here, imagine. Mighty acorns. The shredding eucalyptus. Oysters in the bay. Clouds of swallows circling the Kaiser towers, deliriously. The sun is warm, bland, and the breeze, although smelling slightly foul, is refreshingly cool. She considers walking down through the Laney College campus to the Oakland Estuary where there's a tiny park with a concrete ramp for the launching of small boats. But, unlike Jack London, she has no boat and therefore it's just another dead end. And it's in the opposite direction from the hotel (another dead end), and she'll get wiped out walking back. Or jump into the Estuary, but there'd be no glory in that—it would just be stupid. Try to think of the least stupid thing you could do right now. Look on the bright side. Anything you could think of to do would be less stupid than sitting by Lake Merritt smoking a rolled-up *Wall Street Journal*.

Joggers around the lake, the revolving dead. Don't worry— if anything should by freaky chance come to life in this place They are there with a club to knock it right back out. Everybody either a criminal or a victim, here you get to choose.

Remembering a sunny Sunday afternoon in the early eighties when she'd sailed out of her little apartment (one could still afford an apartment, then) on Telegraph and there's not as soul in sight. Oakland deserted, a twilight zone. She walks down Telegraph; a few cars driving by, the ubiquitous liquor stores open, no people. Then she walks past a bar, and there they are!

The bar is jammed tight with people, and they're all screaming! Screaming in there in the dark. Oh well, stranger things have happened. Walk on down the street, pass another bar and it, too, is packed with screaming people. Then she gets it. The Superbowl. The Raiders are playing today in the Superbowl, and everybody in Oakland is watching it on TV. Our town, our wonderful town, our wonderful Raiders. At least they had that, then. What have they got now? Murder Capital of California. Of the country. Of the *world,* for all anybody knows. Because the place is spiritually defunct, and murder means nothing to people who are already dead.

18. Sanity

I wanted to write something about a difficult subject: shit. It seems that we Americans are obsessively concerned with the subject of sanitation, which comes just before sanity in the dictionary, but is a subject which, unlike sanity and even saintliness, is conspicuously ignored in our literature. Due to sacred taboo or merely the limited confines of good taste, or both?

Walking up Fourteenth Street after an hour or rummaging through the 3-for-$1 bins in front of the bookstore, I see an old woman taking a shit in the street between two parked cars. The shit smells terrible. It runs toward the gutter around the woman's ragged sneakers. The old woman grins at me as I walk by. The old woman grinning, a few teeth left in the filthy face, shitting between two shiny, new parked cars, the cars iridescent in the morning sun with their tinted curved windows, tires deeply grooved like the soles of brand-new Reeboks, bumpers undented, doors and windows locked tight against the cruel world, and the old woman grinning guiltily—"I tried to hide, not to do this in public, but there you are watching, I hope you're enjoying it."

Next year, I think, or the year after that, it'll be me, trying to find a place to shit between parked cars.

Always the fear of becoming ridiculous in your own eyes, being trapped without access to the things which everyone around you takes for granted: a drink of water, a place to get warm, a toilet. A toilet of one's own! Another dream at the end of the rainbow.

"Man Shall Not Live On Macaroni'N'Cheese Alone!"

Thus spoke St. Vinnie, whoever the hell *he* was. And at the other end of the block there's good old St. Anthony expounding the benefits of rice'n'beans. Because rice'n'beans would be your daily fare were you stuck over in San Francisco eating at Cheap Tony's every day. If only the two could have gotten together and devised a real *menu* with actual *choices* on it! On the questionable theory that having a choice between rice'n'beans and macaroni'n'cheese is better than no choice at all.

My problem is not so much with lack of choices as with the Russian roulette of food poisoning. But then, what if I'm the only one who ever gets sick eating this stuff? Hideous digestive upsets being one more thing that nobody wants to talk about, if you could ever get anybody at St. Vinnie's to talk rationally about anything. I've noticed that most of the patrons of St. Vinnie's seem to be already drunk when they get there . . . and maybe that's the critical factor. If you're drunk, you can eat the food and not get sick. But if I could afford to be drunk already at eleven in the morning, I wouldn't *need* to eat at St. Vinnie's. I could either buy real food or just stay drunk all the time and not eat at all. (And then you die!)

I hurry back to the hotel every time I eat at St. Vinnie's. I don't want to risk an attack of food poisoning in the street. You do not want to get sick in the street. What would I do—lie there on the sidewalk while people hopped over me with little exclamations of disgust? Until I gathered enough strength to roll out of sight under a parked car or something, hopefully one whose owner carried insurance? And forget about coming to in a clean, white hospital bed. More likely it would be that room at the jail where they hose down the winos.

Not me. I want to get sick in my own familiar old filthy hall toilet with the familiar old bloodstains on the wall.

(There is a huge old bloodstain running down the wall of the hall toilet in the hotel. One day I mentioned it to Jessy:

"There's this bloodstain on the wall in the toilet. It's always been there. You get used to it."

JESSY: "Is it at wrist-level or throat-level?"

ME: "Wrist level. Uh . . . unless you're sitting down."

The bloodstain splashes all the way down the wall to the floor. Whatever blood was on the floor was mopped up. Or tracked around the halls until it disappeared [like the Cat Star]).

So I was dismayed to find one morning that my own private communal filthy toilet down the hall had ceased to function. It was full, clogged, overflowing with shit. Great. Now I'll have to use that other filthy communal toilet that all those losers at the other end of the hall use.

I'd noticed that it hadn't been cleaned in days, and assumed that the toilet-cleaning maid was no longer with us, probably packed up and fled in the night, certainly violating parole and probation and whatever else had led her into this cesspool in the first place. One is always tempted in such circumstances to simply obtain cleaning supplies and try to stay on top of the mess oneself, but this way lies madness. I know from experience.

The toilet down the hall is also clogged and overflowing. It figures. Probably couldn't handle the extra traffic. OK. I'll just run up one flight of stairs and . . . it's beginning to look serious. This one up here is so bad that the stuff is actually being tracked down the hall carpet. Brown footprints. The smell is beginning to get to me. I go back down two flights to the floor below ours. This one looks like it's full of . . . it can't be. Blood? Did somebody *die* in here? An abortion? A hemorrhage? It certainly looks like an awful lot of. . . .

Back in the room, a bit dizzy, I have to lie down for a few minutes. Funny how a stupid little thing like this can get you totally unstrung, detached from "reality." But somebody did this, some person actually went around and ripped the flushing mechanism out of every toilet in the hotel. Maybe the same pissed-off tenant or ex-tenant who set the fire on the fifth floor. Maybe the ex-maid did it. We'll never know. We are at the mercy of insane forces.

Beset by cramps, I walk three blocks to the BART station. Some of the stations have their "public" toilets inside the paid area, but fortunately this isn't one of them. I'll alternate this facility with the one in the main library (which they keep locked, but they'll usually let you have the key). There is also one at Jack London Square, and possibly the main post office (but probably not) and I'm sure there are others I can get to. You can't use the same one too often.

It'll probably take Them days to get the plumbing at the hotel fixed (it does.) Eat carefully and try not to get food poisoning again before then — *that* would be hellish.

And whatever you do, don't panic.

Repeat after me.

Sanity is next to sanitation.

Sanitation is next to sanity.

Sanitation is next to saintliness.

Other Hotels

I went around to several other hotels in Oakland, and a few in Berkeley (how I would love to move back to Berkeley!) and got absolutely nowhere. I'd ask the Desk Guy if they had a vacancy. He'd tell me I had to talk to the manager. When would the manager be in? I would ask. "Never," would be the reply. Some of them just simply said that they had no vacancies. Maybe they didn't, how would I know? Some of them gave me application forms to fill out. I filled them out and left them at the desk. I never heard from them. Does this mean that I can't move away from Dudley and his room, even if I can't stand it any more?

I can't help wondering what the deal is. Do you have to pay them off? If so, which one? Or all of them? And how much? Do they just not rent to women? Is there some rule written in a book somewhere? Do you have to be a whore? Do you have to belong to some man? Or is it something about *me,* as an individual, personally? Won't somebody *please* tell me? *What* is the fucking *deal?*

Dudley never has a problem getting one of these sleazy hotel rooms. Why? I wish I had the resources and the energy to find out. "Discrimination in Sleazy Hotel Room Rentals? We Shall Not Allow It!" But I don't and I don't. I'm tired. I'm sick and tired. I know I'm being classified as somebody's idea of an undesirable, undesirable even as a tenant of sleazy hotels. But why? What are the secret criteria? Why am I unacceptable? I don't even have a police record. (Maybe that's it!) And plus I'm quiet and nice, and I don't do crazy things, and I don't even take drugs anymore. But I couldn't even try to find out why they wouldn't rent me a room. (There probably *is* something horribly wrong with me, personally, that They can sense.) I'd probably wind up on some super shit list and have to live in a doorway somewhere forevermore.

This makes me feel so trapped and helpless that I can't stand to pursue it. I had the cash. I had the proof of income, proof that I can afford the rent. I found a room in Berkeley for only seventy bucks a week. It looked like a jail cell, except that they let you in and out (most of the time). But they wouldn't rent it to me. If I can't figure out why, I must be abysmally stupid. I filled out the application form (an *application form* for a sleazy room like a jail cell, only without a toilet!). I left the form with them. They said they would let me know if I qualified. (*Qualified!*) They never did. If I, with fourteen years of college and no police record don't qualify, then who does? And I've tried *so hard* to be good. For what? To have to live in a doorway somewhere, or under a freeway overpass, or *what??*

The Cussing Lady

She usually sleeps in a doorway by the Mailbox/UPS place on 13th Street between Franklin and Broadway. She has many bags, and some kind of tarp to use as a tent. When she starts cussing in her shrill grating voice, you can hear her for blocks. And she usually cusses all day, every day. She doesn't seem to cuss people out individually; she simply cusses out the whole world in general.

Drinking coffee in the morning at the coffee place where the *Oakland Trib* people hang out, Ashby sees the Cussing Lady across the street in a niche by the stairs to the three-level parking garage which occupies the whole block of Franklin between 13th and 14th Streets. A very dirty little old lady; she wears a curly black wig, usually askew. She gets kicked out of her doorway every morning when the Mailbox/UPS place opens and relocates herself and her bags to the other side of the street. She isn't cussing this morning—too early for her, maybe. She has her bags gathered around her and is trying to unfold her tarp, which apparently can only be folded and unfolded along established creases, like a giant road map. By the time Ashby has finished her coffee and is leaving the coffee shop, the Cussing Lady has finished the complicated process of unfolding and arranging the tarp so that it covers everything except her feet. A stream of urine runs from beneath the tarp, between her filthy bare feet and across the sidewalk, into the gutter. Office workers hop over the stream with disgusted exclamations.

The Cussing Lady hasn't even started cussing yet.

19.
The Museum

Hanging in the Oakland Museum are paintings at which I could stare for hours, but I feel uncomfortable in there, as though I were being watched, as though someone is afraid that I might touch something or steal something or lapse into some other form of bad behavior.

There are usually very few people in the art section—the groups of schoolkids who are dragged in to look at the stuffed bobcats and old fire engines in the other parts of the Museum never make it as far as the paintings—which is why I enjoy the art exhibit more than anything else except the jade snuffboxes.

I actually like the Museum's art collection, though it would probably be looked down on by almost everyone else in the world. The Museum itself is built according to some California-Weird architectural idea, and it's true that the idea of a museum in California, *anywhere* in California, is weird in itself because the history, in people-terms at least, only goes back about a hundred years, when they had some cowboys and some whores and some opium-smoking Chinese working on the railroad.

I spent a good part of my childhood in New York's Museum of

Natural History, which was a great place for kids in those days and one of the only things New York City had going for kids when it had free admission. And I spent a lot of my adolescence in the N.Y. Metropolitan Museum of Art (also free) where I used to go instead of high school. Compared to these immense immovable monuments, the Oakland Museum is a sort of combination of the Parking Garage School and a sixth-grader's conception of the hanging gardens of Babylon. (Of course, part of it is a parking garage, which they may have just enlarged and extended to include exhibits.)

If the Oakland Museum had chosen to present all of its specimens in diorama form like the Museum of Natural History does (or did), the paintings I like to look at could serve as backdrops. They are fairly large landscapes, or Westernscapes, of looming mountains and vast wildernesses and stormy seacoasts. Luminous and corny, yes, and I'm sure any museum of larger than local repute *would* consider them background material if anything at all. But they are one of the few things I come in contact with which might someday lead me to consider the idea that there might be a God. If I look at one of them as though I were the artist, which I often do, where would I be? Lashed halfway up a vertical sea cliff (with my equipment) at night in the middle of a horrible storm, just out of reach of the flying frozen spray and sixty-mile-an-hour winds? Great! Only God could paint under those conditions.

Contemplating God, I sit on the concrete lip of the fish pond outside the front entrance of the Museum. They let you sit here. I usually bring lunch, a roll or a donut from St. Vinnie's. The pool is long and shallow, with several separate sections, and seems comfortable enough for the carp and turtles which live there. Some of the carp are enormous, and they all have names. I only know the names of a few of them.

The day is mild and weakly sunny; there are few people about. As I sit quietly, throwing bits of crust to the carp, I see two children hesitantly approach the pool about twenty feet away. They are boys, black, maybe nine or ten years old. They don't see me, although they are furtively scanning the area apparently for grownups or any authority figure whose job it would be to give them a hard time. They must be up to no good, sneaking around, obviously expecting to get rousted. I know they're not where kids are supposed to be right now. They're not with any school group, and children almost never come to the museum voluntarily.

They are whispering to each other, still glancing over their shoulders. They sit down together on the lip of the pond, casually, as though they suddenly had permission to be there, belonged there, were *told* to sit there and would not think of disobeying. Amazing, the way children can instantly assume an attitude of innocence, of docility, of harmlessness, like plants. Are they going to poison the fish? Snatch a purse? Rob the gift shop? I shrink behind my pillar. They might decide they can't allow a witness to live.

Now one of them is reaching for something inside his jacket, while the other watches his companion's back. The coast is clear. The kid pulls out what looks like a small mayonnaise jar. Now he, too, is looking around as though afraid of sudden interruption at the very last minute. I focus on the jar. Inside the jar, which is full of water, swims a small goldfish. Suddenly the kid unscrews the lid and dumps the goldfish into the pond. He quickly returns the empty jar to its hiding place. The kids are both looking down into the pond.

"'Bye, Freddy," one calls wistfully.

"Have a nice life, Freddy," calls the other, waving.

They get up and walk away together rather quickly, hurrying back to school or wherever it is that kids are supposed to be at this time of day. The Children Whose Mom Wouldn't Let Them Have A Goldfish, I think of them as, when I think of them. Who will certainly grow up to be monsters like me.

20.

Jump Scene

'Tis the season to be jolly.

God, I *hate* the holidays! The phony Jesus crap, the Real People wallowing in good will and gadgets and Family Values, the sappy music, the worn-out images, the dead trees in the gutter afterward. The TV commercials more than at any other time a long list of all the things you can't have.

"I don't suppose we could get a break from the TV for a little while." I have been unsuccessfully trying to blot out the sound by stuffing wads of tissue in my ears, jamming a pillow over my head.

"No."

"If I have to listen to *Winter Wonderland* one more fucking time. . . ."

"Don't listen."

"Easy for you to say. Sometimes I wish I was deaf."

"What?"

"*Never mind!*" Leap out of bed and get dressed, grab my bag, go out and walk around in the epileptic streets. Dazzling lights, agitated crowds, stupid music blasting. Store windows jammed with "gift suggestions." Blitzed trees wired with flashing bulbs. Baby Jesus. Phony snow. Sleigh bells and Santa Claus. At the MacArthur Mall they had a black woman Santa Claus. That's progress! A cheerful thought to take back to the room. That and a bottle of wine, maybe. . . .

They have been arguing for days.

    This place really sucks.

    So move.

    How come *you* can't move? Why should *I* move?

    Why should *I* pay most of the rent?

    This miserable, miserable place!

    A hundred bucks a week for this. They could at least send up some heat.

    Better than the street, isn't it?

    The street's free, at least. I could get a one-way ticket with the hundred bucks. Go somewhere.

    Where?

    Anywhere.

    Or give it to him so *he* could go somewhere. The fucker. Maybe he wouldn't come back. Sometimes I hate him so much I could kill myself just to get rid of him. To get rid of all of them.

He stands at the sink in the corner, brushing his teeth. Whatever teeth he has left.

    "Why bother?" she says from the bed.

    "What?"

    "Nothing, asshole."

    "Go to sleep."

    "Fuck you." She rolls over to stare out the window. Fucking city lights in a poison cloud. They sleep as far from each other as possible in the bed. How should I do it? If I had a gun. If I had some drugs. If I had some drugs I wouldn't want to kill myself right now, though. If I had bus fare I could go somewhere. Go to the bridge, jump. Jump.

• • •

"If we have to sleep in the same bed, you could at least fuck me sometimes," she had said once, months before. Rolled toward him, put her hand on his arm, on the sleeve of his pajamas. "Want to?"

"No."

"Why not?"

"Go to sleep."

"But why not?"

He rolls over, facing away. "Even if you were young and good-looking I wouldn't want to."

"It's dark."

"It's too much work."

"Thanks so much."

"Let me go to sleep, will you? Just stay on your side of the fucking bed."

He turns off the water. She watches as he puts the top back on the toothpaste and screws it tight. Places the tube and the brush carefully on the shelf, arranged just so. Folds the greasy towel carefully on the rack. She crawls out of bed and out the window. "This is just the end, the ass-end," she says to herself, sitting on the ledge in the dark with her legs dangling four stories above the street. She sits there quietly, smiling, waiting for some signal.

Jump.

Not yet.

Now or never.

Not yet.

Behind her, inside the room, he keeps saying, "Aren't you going to come in now? It's stupid to sit out there. What if somebody sees you?"

"I don't care," she says. "Leave me alone, you son of a bitch."

She feels a sense of real freedom now, a sense of being between two worlds and subject to the laws and follies of neither.

I was writing about choice. To have the power to make a choice which is important and has real meaning. I feel like all the choices I am offered are the equivalent of those triangularly-wrapped sandwiches that are available in a basket on the counter of the candy stand in the bus station at three A.M. You get to choose between rotten egg salad and dried-up cheese. What kind of choice is that? What the fuck kind of choice is *that?* And those are the *positive* choices!

"Please come in now. *Are* you going to come in? Are you going to sit there all *night?*" he is saying, back in the room.

"Maybe," she says, to infuriate him. Maybe if I infuriate him enough he'll give me a shove, and the choice will be his, because I'm too chickenshit to make the choice and I know it, and maybe he has more guts than I do, but I doubt it.

And what about the negative choices? The lesser-of-two-evils choices? And the useless decisions. Like, should I get up in the morning or should I even bother. Should I just lie in bed all day staring at the ceiling. What difference does it make? Who cares? I don't. If I don't even care, who would?

"If you don't come back in this room, I'm calling the police," he says.

She starts laughing. Walk two blocks to the pay phone (the one in the lobby out of order as usual) and then what?

HIM (into phone): "My girlfriend is gonna commit suicide."
PHONE (a recording): "You have reached nine one one. All our lines are busy please stay on the line your call will be answered in the order. . . ."

But he wouldn't hang up, not him. He has put in his two dimes and he's going to stand there until he gets an answer because he thinks that if he hangs up his two dimes won't be returned. Not that he gives a shit about the money. But he has marshalled his energy and his thoughts, in order to communicate a message over the phone, and he is going to convey the message to the proper authority if he has to stand there *all fucking night.*
PHONE (a recording.): "You have reached nine one one. If this is an emergency call please stay on the line. If this is not an emergency you should

call your police at (number) or your fire department at (number) or. . . ."

HIM: "Hello? Hello?" He stands there listening. Oh shit. OK, so she jumped already, and when I get back to the hotel there'll be all these ambulances and flashing lights . . . or maybe they didn't show up yet and there's a little crowd standing around looking down at the . . . or maybe no one saw or heard and I get back and there's just this . . . lying there . . . dead on the sidewalk . . . real dead body. . . .

PHONE: "Nine one one can I help you?"

HIM: "Is this a recording?"

PHONE: "No, sir. What seems to be the problem. . . ."

HIM: "My girlfriend is committing suicide."

PHONE: "Has she taken pills?"

HIM: "No ma'am. I mean, yes. I mean, she takes pills all the time. Lots of pills. But no, she didn't take any pills. I don't think. I don't know."

PHONE: "What kind of pills did she take?"

HIM: "Who knows? Pills. All kinds. White ones and red ones and—"

PHONE: "Is she unconscious, sir?"

HIM: "Oh, hell no. She's sitting on the fucking *window* ledge."

PHONE: "Is this the window ledge at your residence, sir?"

HIM: "My what? My *what?*"

PHONE: "Is she threatening to jump from the ledge, sir?"

HIM: "Oh god."

PHONE: "And what is the address, sir?"

HIM: "The Pits Hotel, 134 East 13th—"

PHONE: "We *know* where it is, sir. We'll send a unit as soon as one is avail—"

HIM: "No, wait! You don't *understand!*"

PHONE: "We'll send a unit as soon as—"

He slams down the phone.

She is still laughing, sitting on the ledge, about two inches from some irrevocable fate. He is standing in the room behind her, threatening to call the police.

"Go ahead, *call* them," she says, laughing. "Fuck. I'll call them myself. *I'm gonna jump!*" she suddenly screams. "I'm gonna fucking jump out this window! Then you'll be sorry. You'll all be sorry." She is sobbing now. "They'll all be fucking sorry. Sorry fuckers. Son of a bitches!"

She waits.

Dudley waits.

Nothing happens.

She climbs back in the window, lies down on the bed, sobbing. "Motherfucking son of a bitches. Motherfuckers. Fuck them. Let *Them* jump."

21.

The Projects

Journal Entry: The H. Hotel, one diagonal block from mine, shows no signs of repairs being made except for tarps over some of the blown-out windows.

It burned (spectacularly, they say; it made the TV news) about two months ago. The top two floors were gutted, but people are still living in the rest of the building, paying rent. The building was apparently never condemned and is still under management by Patels.

An article in the *Trib* yesterday about another hotel a few blocks away, which was closed down after the '89 earthquake and never repaired: people are living there—squatters—without lights or plumbing. This is true of at least half a dozen old hotels around here, also office buildings and abandoned storefronts. In the case of this particular hotel, the owner says that the City refused to OK his petitions to make repairs. The City says his papers were not filed, or filed improperly. Obviously the City is trying to get rid of its poorest citizens, or at least get them out of the downtown area. According to this article, people evacuated from this place after the earthquake were supposed to be able to relocate with Section 8 vouchers. But in order to get a voucher, one had to prove that one had been living there, and most people lost or left their rent receipts behind when they were evacuated.

The article places the number of homeless in Oakland at 5,000, that they *know* of. This may not sound too bad, but if they counted the borderline homeless, like myself, the number would be really appalling.

The lowest-common-denominator approach to the housing problem, or to "problem" housing, seems designed to achieve maximum control over the population and no matter if the conditions insult and outrage everybody. Having spent part of my later childhood in a low-income housing "project" in New York City, I am not entirely ignorant of the protocols.

You have to keep a tight lid on the can, to keep the crap from spilling over into nice neighborhoods.

The more you treat people like garbage, the more they will act like garbage.

Most people have no idea how to act in most situations, and will respond to and follow examples given, willingly or not.

We were angry and frightened to begin with, and had no idea what to do, and were told that we were stupid idiots and worthless scum, and then They expected us to leap up and salute the flag.

The job of sitting on the lid isn't anybody's idea of paradise either. I wouldn't do it. You couldn't pay me enough. I lived in this housing "project" for five or six years, and I got to know maybe four or five of the other tenants in a building seventeen stories high with eight apartments on each floor.

One of the fellow tenants I got to know was Mr. Washington, who sat on the lid for free. A legless veteran of World War One, he parked his wheelchair at the doorway of our building every day, all day and sometimes far into the night. He'd keep track of everybody who went in or out, what everyone was doing, who was up to no good, and basically everything that went on. I used to keep him company on warm evenings, just to have somebody to talk to. I liked him; I thought he was a cool old guy.

The projects must have been better in those days than they are now. There was no security gate in the lobby of the building, no armed guard. The lobby was just an empty space where the mailboxes were, leading to the elevators and the stairwells. There were two elevators: one stopped on the even-numbered floors and one on the odd. They were small self-service elevators; their metal interiors were painted a horrid fleshy pink and smelled like a public toilet. If the elevator which was supposed to stop on your floor was broken, not an infrequent occurrence, you were supposed to take the other one to the floor above and run down a flight of stairs. But you stayed out of the stairwells if you could.

The hallways had walls of beige tile, long and narrow and windowless. The apartment doors were metal. The walls of our apartment were some kind of metal, so you couldn't bang in a nail, or even a thumb tack, to hang things up. It was against the rules to hang things on the walls. I found some double-sided tape which worked pretty well, and some stick-on hooks, and we used those. The walls were all painted the same dull pukey green. Tenants weren't allowed to paint over it. If ever at some time in the future we needed a new paint job, the Housing Authority informed us, we could fill out a form and eventually the City would come in and slap on a new coat of dull pus-green.

My family had a two-bedroom apartment. If my sister had been a boy, we'd have been issued a three-bedroom unit. What I wanted most in the whole world was to have my own room. What my sister wanted most was to have a dog. No dogs were allowed either, so I guess we were evenly dealt our disappointments.

I didn't hate the projects. My family considered itself lucky to get a project apartment after living in an abandoned building on Manhattan Avenue with no heat or hot water. In the projects, the City turned off the heat only between ten P.M. and seven A.M. We didn't complain.

Like the hotel, the project was lowest-common-denominator housing. There was a sense of danger, if you can use the word without implying excitement or mystery. There was no mystery or excitement involved. Just a continuous dull "watch-your-back" feeling which drained your energy and eventually turned you into a predator or prey. We were prey. We were rats in a maze with nobody monitoring our behavior unless we broke the rules.

After a while we realized that you could break the rules if you could do it quietly, without attracting Their attention or being obnoxious about it. Like the family across the hall from us who kept chickens in their apartment. They could have gotten away with it except for one really loud and annoying rooster who insisted on crowing at dawn every morning, piercingly and at length, so that everybody in the building could hear him. This must have been their prize fighting cock, probably an important source of income for them, but my family was ignorant of things like chicken-fighting and we wondered why they didn't just eat the son of a bitch. We didn't complain because of the risk of attracting Their attention.

But somebody complained, and the chicken-keepers were evicted. Everyone was glad to see them go. This was not the case, however, when the City announced that it was evicting Mr. Washington. It seemed that the old man's wife, who had remained mostly bedridden in their apartment, had died. They had been married for fifty or so years, and Mr. Washington was devastated. Then the City declared that the old man, as a single individual, was no longer eligible for a project apartment and he had to get out. Everybody liked Mr. Washington, and there was talk of protest, a petition, stuff like that. But the tenants finally did nothing, afraid of getting their own names on the project shit list as troublemakers and candidates for the boot. One morning on my way to school the City men were carrying Mr. Washington's belongings out of the building and putting them on the curb. When I got home from school they were gone. Someone said he'd been put in a "home." After his departure, the crime rate in the building soared through the roof.

22.
Death

Because poverty is boring. The endless struggle to pay the rent is boring. Because you hate the dump where you live. Why struggle to pay rent for a place to live if you're not living? As though you're already dead, and have to pay rent on your own grave. Worse, you have to pay it to the ones who killed you. And They didn't kill you for personal reasons, or because you were some enemy of Theirs, They just wanted to profit from your misery.

To avoid the horrors of the Street. Why should They care how horrible it has become, that it is becoming worse all the time? They never see it, or if They do it is from inside the shiny metal shell of a new car.

I walk to St. Vinnie's today because I can't spare the bus fare. I have only enough money left for cigarettes and wine. I try to enjoy my walk, a round-trip of almost thirty blocks, but the day is gray and depressing. The whole downtown area looks like a trash heap. Whole buildings are still boarded up from the earthquake. Human wrecks huddle in doorways, chilled. Ragged pigeons flap around aimlessly.

I am hungrier than usual and the food looks OK. The nuns are smiling and cheerful, reeling with visions of heaven. It is the end of the month and the place is crowded with families whose checks have run out. The children are silent and depressed; the women tired and grim.

I should have taken the hint. I barely make it back to the Funky Hilton before being brought to my knees with cramps. I crawl into the filthy toilet and writhe there, thankful that at least I made it back, that I have a toilet to writhe upon. But the cramps become so awful that I pray to die. I promise never to eat at St. Vinnie's again, to never eat anything at all again. I have an excruciating thirst, and cold sweat drips from my face and forms a puddle at my feet. I must be in shock. But the pain doesn't lessen. I twist around so as to vomit in the bowl instead of on the floor; there is no sink in the toilet. No relief of cold water on the face, the wrists, the back of the neck. There are chunks of macaroni in my hair.

I crawl back to the room and lie on the floor without the strength to even turn on the shower or heave myself over the lip of the little sink.

"You're white as a sheet," says Dudley. "Are you OK?"

Right! "Go get me a bottle of wine," I croak. "Now. Please."

Dudley brings me the wine, from the corner store. In a while I feel a bit better. I wash the vomit out of my hair and fall on the bed.

"You threw up in your hair!" Dudley scolds. "That's disgusting."

"I'll never eat at St. Vinnie's again," I say. "Better to starve." I drink the whole bottle of wine before going to sleep for fourteen hours.

"I thought you weren't going to ever wake up," are Dudley's first words when I open my eyes the next day.

"I wish I hadn't," I say. I get up to wash my sweated-out clothes in the bucket in the shower.

I had a series of death dreams. For three nights in a row, each night a dream about death, which clung to me all of the next day. If I were superstitious I would take this as a sign of something, my own immediate demise being the most reasonable assumption. Good thing I'm not superstitious.

I can't remember the content of the dreams, just the substance:

The dream of the first night was about the finality of death.

The second night's dream involved the witnessing of a death (not my own).

The third explained the inevitability of death.

Statement of fact: Everybody dies.

Dream: I don't care about everybody. *I* don't want to die.

Rationalization: If you *didn't* die, wouldn't you get terribly bored eventually?

Dream: That's so glib and stupid I can't believe you said it! You just don't *understand!*

The main fear these dreams inspire is that I won't be able to recover from the impact of my own emotions, and will just go on wailing and sobbing and spinning in a bottomless pit.

But in some way I *knew* I was dreaming, and had maybe asked for these experiences and let myself get swallowed in them; that these realizations and this knowledge are necessary equipment for survival at the level in which I find myself. Will they make me better and stronger? Only if I can escape them by understanding them and encompassing them and incorporating them into my thinking processes.

Bare emotions are part of the basic equipment of life as we know it. Animals mourn and grieve. If you can't get past this stuff you have to stop, observe your reactions, try to understand and control them. Equipment is useless if you don't know how to use it, and worse than useless if you can't use it *and* can't get rid of it.

Maybe just the fact that I've been able to remember these feelings and drag them out into the cold light of day will be useful.

I am usually pretty hard on myself this way. To kick and poke at one's basic fears is stressful and damaging, but to back off and avoid them is worse in the long run. Now that I'm old enough to know how long the long run is.

To say "I won't forget this" is not the same as saying "What if I don't forget this?" thereby questioning one's ability to deal with one's own reactions and creating anxiety. Instead, say "I certainly won't forget this, you fucker!" Bring in the element of anger and arm yourself for a fight. Don't delude yourself into thinking the war is over. If it's an unwinnable war, remember that in a war against yourself, if you can't win you can't lose either. Flip side of the same war. Which is going to continue whether you choose to participate or not. And you might as well participate, since it's the only action around right now. Even if it is only a cheap, cheesy cold war in your head.

Maybe my unconscious self put me through this dream process because I've been savoring the idea of suicide too much. When I feel like I'm being sucked into some sort of irreversible, doomed existence, a voice in my head says (tearfully and histrionically), "Just fucking *kill* yourself and put an end to it all!" And another voice says, "Why not?" And a third voice says "*Wait* a minute! Who the fuck do you think you are to tell *me* what to do?"

So I had this other dream, which I will call the *Swimming in Shark-Infested Waters* dream: I am standing on a balcony or deck at night, looking down into a shallow, shark-infested lagoon. A small animal, a dog I think, has fallen into the water, and is being attacked by sharks. One leg is bitten off, and the dog swims around in circles with the remaining three, snarling and snapping and trying to bite the sharks. Then another leg is eaten. Then the tail. Finally, nothing is left but the trunk and the head, which is still spinning and growling and trying to bite. A voice says to me: "There's no point in giving up until you have absolutely nothing left to fight with." I wake up hearing these words, which I have been unable to forget.

It would be nice to believe in a god, or gods, or heaven and hell, or reincarnation, or a spirit world, or past lives, or an alternate universe or a great beyond of some sort. But if you don't, I suppose this life is the only one you get. And the words are singularly appropriate: "Why give up until you have nothing left to fight with?"

It is either very late at night, or very early in the morning. Ashby walks down the train tracks on Second Street, where the freight trains unload fresh vegetables and fruit and other goods to the distributors every morning. The street is totally empty of people and traffic, and the warehouses are dark and empty.

She hears the rumbling of a train in the distance, sees its headlight far off down the street. She climbs up onto one of the waist-high loading platforms and sits down against the wall of a warehouse among some empty boxes. She lights a cigarette.

The train comes steadily, moving at perhaps fifteen miles an hour, travelling north. Its headlight, single eye, pierces the blackness of the deserted street.

"I am not going to think about throwing myself in front of that train," she thinks. "Throwing myself in front of that train is absolutely the last thing on my mind, at this point in time. I do not intend to establish a personal relationship with that train, or make it in any way aware of my presence."

I realize that just being in this desolate no-man's-land, this godforsaken urban wasteland, alone in the middle of the night, is suicidal. Fortunately, I have the power (at times like this) to make myself invisible. Of course!

The train rumbles past, maybe eight feet away. I cup my cigarette and sit still, hidden in the shadows of the boxes.

Journal Entry: I've been getting so much better. I am getting so much better that I can lay awake (lie awake?) for a half hour or more before my mind starts spinning away into the horrors. Sometimes it doesn't even start spinning . . . if I take my pills. I can take pills and keep my mind out of the shit until the pills knock it out. It. My mind. I have to lean on it a little sometimes. I have to lean on my own mind. I have to hold heavy threats over my mind sometimes. I tell It: "You *will not* think any bad stuff tonight!" I tell It: "If you think any bad stuff, if you even *think* about thinking bad unpleasant things tonight, *I will kill you!*" And somehow It seems to know that I'm serious, that I really mean what I'm saying. My own mind is afraid of me.

The Vision of the Creature

Time to play. You are sinking into sleep. Losing control. You are power-less to stop the process. It is coming up to meet you. From the depths of your head. You can't stop it; it's time to play.

You are in a small boat, bobbing in the midst of trackless ocean. You, and the others in the boat, possess spears and sharp sticks. Your mon-ster has already appeared: a wall of white wrinkled substance, feature-less, 20 feet wide and 20 feet high.

You are rowing toward it in your little wooden boat. It rises up from the ocean waters in confrontation. You stick your spear into the midst of the blank and eyeless face. You are holding a rope which is at-tached to the end of the spear. With a great upheaval of cold ocean, the wall sinks beneath green heaving surface of water and sky. Suddenly all is still, except for heaving surfaces and shrieks of sky creatures.

Your flimsy boat rides on a thin skin of sea; solid land is miles below. You peer over the side of your skiff, down into the cold green depths of that upon which you float like a bit of debris in a storm.

You look straight down into the shadowy pit over which you are miraculously buoyed by you-know-not-what tenuous power of some strange god, and what is it that you see below? Far far below, a tiny wa-vering shape which remains in the same spot, growing in size as you watch. Petrified, you watch. Out of the green depths it seems to be float-ing up toward you from below, aimed at your very substance and bow-els. From below it grows, blossoming into a larger and more terrible shape. Swimming straight up from the unimaginable deep green, and you know that you have blown your only chance to meet the monster head-on.

Like a freight train it is coming now. Your feet grow numb with anticipation, then your legs, your hips, your bowels clench in awful anticipation and your breathing constricts. It comes.

And you had always expected death from above. Death crashing down on a defenseless head, angels and demons swooping, stooping from above, how much better than this horrible rushing destruction rising from below—how much more merciful to have the eyes blanked out first, and the ears, and all the senses of the brain!

And now the monstrous jaw opens in anticipation. Will it snap shut before you are flung into the ruthless sky?

Love Notes

Home, home of the strange
Where the pimps and the crack-monsters stay
Where your money's all spent
After you pay the rent
And they treat you like shit anyway.

I wrote this song one night because I thought the hotel, like the Love Boat, should have a theme song.

I'd been finding little notes shoved under the room door in the mornings when I woke up. Small, torn fragments of paper with scribbling on them—not real writing but the sort of scrawls an illiterate would make to imitate writing. Occasionally I'd find a picture of a naked woman, torn from a magazine, with the note. The pictures were never pornographic, just the kind of standard nudie pin-up photos like you'd find on an old calendar from the fifties.

Sometimes, when Dudley was working swing or graveyard shift, I'd hear a tiny tap on the door. I'd yell "Who the fuck is it?" and there'd be no answer. I'd look down at the base of the door and there'd be a little scribbled-on scrap of paper. One time I had enough nerve to leap off the bed and yank the door open. Nobody; the whole length of the hall silent and empty. A little scribbled note at my feet, scotch-taped to a naked-lady photo.

I showed the notes and pictures to Dudley. He laughed.

"Somebody likes you," he said with a stupid grin.

Suddenly I was furious. "That's not even funny!" I yelled. I wadded up the notes and threw them on the floor. "Not fucking funny! I'm not amused! Look at this!" I picked one up and flattened it out, held it up for him to look at. "This is not even dirty. I could understand something dirty. A proposition, a love note, a beaver shot, a dirty *drawing,* even. But this is just sick! Sick! Now I have to deal with *this* fucking lunatic on top of everything else!" I picked up the bits of paper and tore them into smaller bits and threw them out in the hall.

Dudley shrugged. "Just another nut." He turned on the TV.

I retreated to my corner of the bed and positioned my paperback book in front of my face to blot out the world. I am horribly spooked.

After this, when Dudley worked nights I chained the door and stayed awake until he came "home." I listened for the tap on the door. I realized that my attempt to surprise the note-sender by yanking open the door to catch him in the act had been nuts. What if I *had* caught him out there? What would I have *done?*

"Kicked his ass," I muttered to myself. But I knew I was no longer capable of that. I was scared and had lost the edge that anger would provide. Plus, I was in danger of expecting Dudley to flesh out some illusion of security which I seemed to need, and that was something I'd promised myself I'd never do.

A few weeks later the notes stopped appearing, but I was deeply demoralized by then.

"Get any love letters this week?" Dudley would joke.

I was too demoralized to think of a snappy reply. All I could come up with was, "What kind of sick jerk would send love notes to a bag lady?"

Then I thought: It's only a matter of time before I'll begin to miss the love notes and hope they'll start reappearing. I probably should have been flattered and accepted them as a compliment.

For a change of scene, I tack some pretty posters up on the walls of the room. Hoping, I suppose, to achieve some sort of cheery effect, but they only succeed in making the rest of the room look more dismal and shabby than before. I want to tear them down and rip them to shreds, but then I decide to leave them up and give them time to work; some positive transformation may yet take place.

Now I'm waiting and wondering what would happen if I put up some really ugly stuff—would it make the rest of the room look better? But can one get constructive results by being surrounded by ugliness day after day? It's probably worth a try. What if I did both—maybe alternate the beautiful with the ugly, or do one wall of each? Contrast is more important than most people think. Contrast always sets some process in motion, but perhaps not a beneficial process. All I need right now is more negative input.

Dudley came in and said, "How come you put that crap up on the walls? Can't you leave anything alone? I'm getting really really sick of you and your shit."

I was sure he was going to assert his masculine territorial prerogative and order me to take them down, which I would refuse to do, probably precipitating a battle. But he parked himself in front of the TV with his six-pack and didn't say another word.

I stare at the posters, trying to transport my spirit into the worlds they represent, but they seem trite and unimaginative. Cheap posters from the bargain bin. What I need are some really good quality prints that I can get lost in. Plaster the walls and ceiling with them. Dudley would go nuts.

Later, I cried for three or four hours. Silently, mechanically, the tears pouring out as though under pressure with the valve wide open. For no particular reason except Why Me? Poor me. Poor old me. Can't put a poster on the wall without getting rapped out about it. How does one get caught in such a miserable situation? (You put yourself in these situations.) Why do I have to suffer this constant abuse? (You enjoy it.) Why couldn't I have been a Real Person? (You don't *want* to be a Real Person.) I've lived my whole life so far with nothing, *nothing!* (You don't *deserve* anything!) Why *me???* (Because you're weak and stupid and ugly and inferior and fat and repulsive and ignorant and obtuse and selfish and insensitive and blind.) Why do I hate myself? (You hate yourself.) I hate myself. I hate myself. I should die.

I get out of bed with a flood of tears pouring down my face. Dudley, in front of the TV, glances at me, rolls his eyes, shrugs, and goes back to his program. I take down the posters carefully, quietly, deliberately, and one by one tear them into tiny pieces. I kill them so I can survive.

The Howling Guy

On a Wednesday night, around midnight, I am awakened by the sound of a man howling in the street outside the hotel.

"Waaaaaah! Hooo-hooooooo! Bawwwwww!" A man is howling in the street, wailing with the loud uncontrolled grief of a very small child.

I can't see him from the window of the room. My view of the street, out between two arms of the E, is too limited. I can, however, see parts of two police cars, the front end of one and the rear end of another. The wailing echoes down the canyon of the street. Flashing red, yellow, and blue lights are bouncing around on walls and windows. Car doors are heavily slammed, and the sound of running footsteps reverberates.

"Woooo-hooooooo!" wails the guy.

A cop voice yells, "I'm gonna send *you* to the *hospital,* man!"

"Waaaaah!" howls the guy.

Sounds of scuffling, muffled impacts. Car doors open and slam, echoing hollowly. Lights flash, a colorful cop light show projected on the dark silent buildings.

Whoop-Whoooppp! A siren whoops, as though in triumph. I can

sense the whole hotel wake up, all except for Dudley, who sleeps the sleep of the dead, as usual. Echoes bounce and rebound. Whhhoooooppppp!

As though they can't resist waking every single one of us up, gratuitously, before they leave.

The cop cars drive away.

"Thanks a lot, fuckas!" Somebody upstairs hollers out the window.

Later that night I get pissed off enough to write:

The Nomads' Manifesto!

OK. So *what* if we're homeless? When did that become a fucking crime? Maybe we don't *want* to hang "Home Sweet Home" on the wall. Maybe it was never "an option" for us, that we would have that nice little slice of the good old American Dream. If that's true, why shouldn't we just say *Fuck* the American Dream! They won't even let us have a spot to pitch our little tent? Fuck Them! With Their: "We *own* this and this and this and that and blah blah blah! Can't you people see all these fences, the signs, the warnings, the barbed wire? The gates, the locks, the security systems? The alarms, the cameras, the vicious dogs? What's *wrong* with you people? Are you *blind?*" Well, fuck *you!* What if we *like* being homeless, so what? We're Nomads, howz *that?* We *like* filling out forms, standing in line. We simply *love* to eat macaroni'n'cheese, it's our absolute favorite thing! Do you hear us telling *you* what to eat? What to drink? What to smoke? Where to live? *How* to live? Hell no! We respect your right to choose. This is America! We're not homeless, we're Nomads! When They ask us where we live, we don't cringe and say "nowhere," we jump up and yell, *"Everywhere!"* We are exercising our right to be Americans, our right to choose. We have rights, ain't that right? Being Americans and all, like They taught us in school, right? Were They lying? Stand up and tell us They lied, that we got no rights or nothing. Tell us who stole our share of the American bloody Dream and why They were allowed to do it. Tell us that if we don't become just like Them, even though They won't *let* us be like Them, we're doomed to be sucked dry and wiped out by exploiters and greedheads of all nations. Tell us we should eat poison, and drink it and smoke it. Should we listen? Do They expect us to? Who are They, anyway? How *dare* They?

And so on.

I think I'm losing it, *losing* it. Whatever it is.

Another Locked 24.

Room Mystery

One warm California summer evening, a woman checks into a sleazy hotel in a medium-sized California city. We don't know whether or not she used her right name, or if it matters. All we know is that she is young, black, and neatly dressed. She carries a suitcase and a Bible.

She is given a room on the top floor, which is the seventh floor of the hotel. She enters the room, locks the door behind her. She places her room key, her jacket, and her suitcase on the bed. Holding her bible, she walks to the window, opens it, and jumps out.

She lands on the roof of a luncheonette next door to the hotel, which is closed at the time. The body is not discovered for three days, when the hotel manager goes to her room to collect more rent and finds the door locked from the inside. Receiving no reply to his knocking, he summons his wife and they enter the room together. The wife sees the empty room, the wide-open window, says "Oh god," and turns away.

The keys, the jacket, and the suitcase sit on top of the neatly made bed. According to the manager's wife, who makes the beds, this one has been neither slept in nor even sat upon by their departed guest. The manager looks down and sees the body of the woman who will never again have to pay the rent.

This story, as far as I know, never appeared in the media. Dudley told me this story. It happened in the hotel where he lived previous to this. I happened to have paid him a visit the next day, and he showed me the spot where the body had been. We had to lean pretty far out of his window, on the fourth floor.

"There are only a few windows on that side of the building," he pointed out. The roof of the diner was littered with garbage, broken glass, pigeon shit. The death scene was outlined in discarded latex gloves and other cop debris. "I saw all these cops down on the roof," said Dudley. "The body was all bloated up and swollen. It was in the sun for three days. She was still holding her Bible."

Nobody knew who she was or why she jumped.

Looking at that filthy roof, I suddenly flashed on how lovely it would be to jump off the Golden Gate.

Or even the Bay Bridge.

If and/or when I might find it necessary to jump.

Maybe I'm still a romantic.

This story is a ghost which haunts me.

Jack London 25. Square

The square is located at the end of Broadway, where Broadway meets the estuary. On Broadway and Fourteenth Street, winos wearing ragged blankets around their shoulders sit in the shadows of the towering glass slabs of new office buildings. On Twelfth, the luxurious Convention Center with its hi-rise hotel, and a few blocks further the freeway roars overhead.

The children's jail takes up a block of Broadway, down past the freeway. Sometimes when I'm buying a hamburger at the Nathon's across the street, I see Them unloading children from trucks and herding them into the side door of this huge, faceless, concrete bunker. The adult jail is two blocks north. Somewhere under the street is an echoing concrete corridor through which prisoners from the jail are herded to the courthouse, which is south of Broadway. All the roaring machinery of Justice and Death.

At the bus stop across the street from the main police headquarters, a few people who have been visiting the jail, or have been in court, are usually waiting.

Broadway becomes emptier as one nears the square. On weekdays there is a surge of people at noontime, office workers coming down to the square with their bag lunches, to eat their sandwiches by the water under the scrutiny of hungry seagulls.

Across the estuary in Alameda, the Naval Air Station roars. To the north, the huge thundering frameworks of the docks where container-ships are unloaded. Steel spiderweb structures in the smog.

I find my way to Jack London's cabin and sit down on the bench outside. A brass plaque attached to the cabin claims that this is Jack's Original Cabin (or one of them), relocated from its original site in the wilderness of Alaska. There is also a tiny wooden boat in a slimy pond outside one of the Square's seafood restaurants. Whether this is the real "Dazzler" or a replica I do not know.

I like to sit outside the cabin, which looks tiny and shabby enough to be real. The door and the tiny window are covered by metal grilles. Inside are a narrow bunk, table, and chair, crudely fashioned from rough planks. A little iron woodstove sits in one corner. Pennies are strewn on the dirt floor—offerings to Jack pushed though the grilles by tourists.

I like to wonder what Jack would make of his beloved Oakland today. His beautiful oyster-laden bay. I can picture the teenage Jack sailing the Dazzler out into a black storm in the bay on a cold night or riding the top of a freight car through the Sierra snowsheds in a blizzard. Do people still do things like that? I picture myself sitting in the cabin in the blinding wilderness of Alaska, writing by the flickering light of a kerosene lamp. And dead at forty from an overdose of crap.

"If you could have been here now," I tell him, "And lived as long as I have, in the midst of all this shit, you'd be dead."

A young couple, tourists, stroll hand in hand past the bench, peering at the cabin.

HE: "What's *that?* What's that *thing* doing here?"

SHE: "I dunno. Yuck."

They wander off.

Wedding Party at 26. Lake Merritt

I regularly wander down to Lake Merritt now on sunny days, sometimes on chilly or foggy days, mainly because I can't stand to be inside, especially inside the hotel. I like to take a loaf of St. Vinnie's stale bread to feed the birds and a pocket full of nuts or sunflower seeds for the squirrels. A Pepsi and a bag of fries for me, or lately (following some unwritten but well-known pattern?) a bottle of wine or quart of beer or, if short on funds, a tall can of Green Mamba.

I always pass by a house which is in the park between the lakeshore drive and the water, across from the main public library, called the Edgemere House. Once the private residence of a wealthy family, it is now a landmark belonging to the city and free guided tours are shown through it on certain days. It can also be reserved for private parties, wedding receptions, and such.

Not a peaked and gabled lunatic Victorian structure such as one is accustomed to seeing in the area, the Edgemere House is rather stiff and square-shouldered, blocky and precise. Edwardian or Georgian, maybe. Inside the house, which isn't very large, are a lot of too-small rooms (I took the tour once), also stiff and square, stuffed with heavy antique furniture and spindly tables and lamps and knickknacks and whatnots and carved cherubs. As though the people who built it and lived in it were fleeing and hiding from the wild-and-wooly, wide open spaces of the American West.

Today as I pass the house I notice that it is set up for some sort of event, with tables on the back lawn and a multitude of white flowers and ribbons. A wedding party, I assume.

On this particular day I was hoping the Canadian geese would be there again, but they had flown, Lake Merritt being one of the less desirable pit-stops on their migratory itinerary. I walk on along the waterline anyway; you can usually spot something interesting if you're looking.

There seem to be no decent-sized fish left in the lake, as far as anyone knows. Just a lot of tiny minnows that wouldn't make a meal for a mouse. Schools of them by the shore, where the water is a few inches deep. All jerking around in tight harmony, all changing direction at the exact same tenth of a second, nobody knows why. Maybe nobody wants to know why. Jacques Cousteau could explain it, I'm sure. Jacques Cousteau Explores Lake Merritt!

A little kid is watching them, holding the hand of his mom, who is probably afraid he'll jump in if she lets go. He is tugging on her hand, jumping up and down, pointing at the water. He's all excited by the minnows. Little kids often think real life is more interesting than TV. Even the most trivial, ordinary things.

KID: "Mommy, Mommy! How come they all do that? How come they all turn at the same time? How do they know when to all turn at the same time?"

MOM: "I don't know."

KID: "But you're supposed to know! You're supposed to know everything! I bet you know but you won't tell!"

MOM: "I don't."

KID: "You do. Why won't you tell me? I'm your kid! You're supposed to tell me stuff. That's your job."

MOM: (sighs) "OK. See, all those little fish are attached to little strings, right? Only you can't see them. They're like little spider web strings, OK?"

KID: "But Mommy! I can't *see* them!"

MOM: "I *said* you can't see them. Nobody can see them. But they're all attached together, right? All the little fishies. By these little invisible strings."

KID: "Wow!"

MOM: "And there's this bigger fish, out in the lake, and *he* pulls the strings, alright? And they all move together, the little ones, because the Big Guy is out there pulling the strings."

KID: "How big is he?"

MOM: "He's really, *really* big. That's why he stays out in the middle. Because he's really really big."

KID: "As big as Jaws? As big as Godzilla?"

MOM: "Yeah. He's about the same size as Godzilla. That's why he can't come close to the shore where we can see him. Because it's really really deep out there, so there's room for him. And he just sits there pulling the little strings."

The kid stands quietly, for a moment. Then: "Can we go to McDonalds now?" He starts pulling mom off in a different direction. "Can I have a Kiddie Mac?"

I wonder if grown-ups get any points for thinking that sometimes real life is more interesting than television.

A bit later I walk back by the Edgemere House. The wedding party has assembled.

Perhaps a hundred people dressed in gowns and tuxedos, coiffed and jewelled, enveloped in the invisible aura of money. They sit at tables on the back lawn surrounded by cascades of flowers and ribbons and balloons; some wander in and out of the house chattering gaily, holding drinks, laughing, and sparkling. Two of them (which two I couldn't figure out) had just been married. Poor fools. . . .

A chamber music ensemble with recorders and flutes replaces

the string quartet which has been playing on the glassed-in sun porch, and the music is exquisite, lovely, like music you'd hear on the PBS Channel 9, only real.

The people at the tables are being served by uniformed waiters and waitresses. (A waitress stands outside the service entrance, smoking. A wino approaches her and asks her for a cigarette. She gives him one. She lights it for him.) Imported beer and wine, lush salads, thick sandwiches. The back lawn is not very large; it slopes toward the lake and is surrounded by a tall, heavy, spiked wrought-iron fence. The guests seem crowded inside the fence.

I sit on the grass, maybe twenty feet from the fence, listening to the music. About halfway between me and the fence, a skinny, homeless black man sprawls asleep or unconscious on the scraggly grass. I sip my concealed quart of Bud through a drinking straw. (You know you're in a bad neighborhood when the liquor store clerk gives you a free straw with your beer.) A couple of derelicts wander by, automatically ask me for a cigarette. I distribute a few; I have a full pack.

After a while I move a little closer to the fence. The guests are all talking loudly, perhaps unnecessarily so, and I want to listen to the conversations. I think of the image of a zoo; it is They who are in the cage. Loud, young fat men are talking about their investments, their legal or medical practices. Well-preserved old men talk about their golf games and their portfolios; the middle-aged about their insurance packages and European cruises and the kids in grad school.

Some other Lake Merritt regulars have paused in their wanderings to check out the wedding party. A few sit on the grass nearby, mildly interested but not excited; we'd be sitting on the grass somewhere or other anyway, and the music is nice, and it's more interesting than TV. A bag lady rummages endlessly through her bags. A few joggers, even, have interrupted their revolutions to contemplate the spectacle. As the silent crowd grows, the talk of the guests becomes louder. Women talk and talk about their luncheons and their committees and their charity benefits and their museum work.

A mild-looking middle-aged woman, sitting at a table near the fence, has attracted my attention. She smiles at me, makes a little ges-ture. I stare back but do not acknowledge. She points at me, then at the table in front of her where there sits a plate containing a large uneaten sandwich. She assumes that I'm hungry. Maybe it's part of my bag lady gig to be perpetually hungry, I don't know. But I'm not; I'm still faintly queasy from luncheon at St. Vinnie's.

She sneaks a look around to ascertain that no other wedding guest has observed her gesture. Maybe it's in bad taste to take such lib-erties with the host's catered food. She doesn't want to be seen giving me the sandwich, but she wants to be able to talk about it later. Or feel good about it later. How much middle class guilt can be appeased by one sandwich? In such a way as not to be observed from within or with-out, except by me, she eases the plate through the bars and places it on the grass just outside the fence.

She looks at me hungrily, waiting for me to accept her offering. This pisses me off, for some reason, and I turn away. The Deliberate Snub. I conceive the scenario of myself crawling to the food on my hands and knees and cramming it into my mouth like an animal with appropriate slobbering and grunting noises. What I would really like to do is wrap the sonofabitch up and take it "home" for later. But I can't bring myself to do anything. When I turn back to look, the woman is gone but the plate is still there.

A ragged, skeletal, fevered-looking derelict stumbles by.

"Hey, man," I say to this specter. "There's a sandwich over there if you're hungry."

He looks at me, then at the plate. His eyes light up. "Gee wow thanks!" he says. He stumbles toward the fence, falls on his knees, and begins to devour the food with grunting, slobbering noises. I get up and walk away, not looking back.

This whole episode allowed me a feeling of small triumph which lasted about ten minutes, until I stopped to think about this woman. Who had the kindness to notice the less-fortunate stranger outside looking in.

I begin to wonder—what if I were in her position? Would I have shown such generosity of spirit?

I suspect not. I'd probably have turned my back on the whole miserable assortment of dregs and creeps and said, as Dudley would, "Fuck 'em. They get what they get."

27. The Rat Bite

In 1970 I was twenty-five years old, exactly half the age I am now. I had no husband, no job, no marketable skills or social graces, little formal education, no money, and no place to live. I had two small second-generation welfare brats, ages two and four. Fortunately, I had a friend named Adeline, who helped me set up house in Berkeley, which was a good place for small children and refugees from New York City.

When the children were a few years older and enrolled full-time in school, I decided to enroll myself and attempt to secure that prize at the end of the rainbow: a high school diploma. Not that I hadn't figured out along with most of my male counterparts including the ex-father of the children that *you can't support a family on a minimum-wage job,* but I had hope: that insidious poison which encourages one to Do The Best You Can With What You Have And Surely Something Good Will Happen Eventually Maybe.

And maybe eventually something good would happen; maybe by the time the children needed separate rooms you would have achieved the means to provide them. Maybe by the time they're ready for college you'll be able to send them.

But there are all these built-in cutoff points which They've provided to tip the scales against you every time you try to take a step toward that magical point of balance where everything works. And you know they're there, and you may even know where they are, but you think that by the time you reach that point (the point where the children need bus fare and lunch money every day and have to buy their own schoolbooks, for instance) you will have figured out how to provide the extras. And then They cut you off.

They will pay to send you to vocational training, but They will not pay for child care while you go. They will help you find a job, but the job will neither provide nor pay enough for you to provide child care. And then the "taxpayers" vote in an initiative which assures that persons with incomes as low as yours will never be able to afford decent housing in California. Which was supposed to encourage landlords to lower the rent. My landlord doubled the rent. We went on to live in basements, attics, and finally a junked trailer in someone's backyard.

And while you're trying to deal with this the children get older. They need more stuff. They're supposed to go to high school. They get part-time jobs that they hate where the paycheck is deducted from the welfare check. They want nice clothes and sports equipment and stereos. Cars. Their own phones. They're ashamed to have their friends visit. The list of things you can't provide for them gets longer. You can't pay the bills. The rent goes up and up. They hate you. You have failed in life. You are a failure as a parent and a human being. You can't figure out how to go on. You might as well die. And then They cut you off.

But your life is not a failure, you must remind yourself. It is merely the logical extension of having been born poor.

There are advantages, at times, to not being a Real Person. You may have to spend a lot of time looking for them and figuring out how to use them, but they're there. Sometimes you can walk through walls, fit into places where Real People can't fit, go places where Real People don't believe you can go. Sometimes you can fly. But you have to do a lot of crawling first, a lot.

I'd been working on my application to a four-year college. A Real College. If I made it I'd be the first in my immediate family. It's harder that way, having no one who has gone before to help you find the way.

My older child had chosen to go to a community college in another city. He worked weekends, lived with me, and needed eight dollars a day just for bus fare. My younger child, Jessy in this story, was in the middle of her High School Crisis. We'd moved from her former school district, and the former school wouldn't allow her to continue there. She dropped out. I dragged her to the new school she'd been assigned to.

A bleak, dirty brick building rising in the middle of a vast trash-covered concrete yard, surrounded by razor wire.

"I'm not going," she said after one look.

"I guess not," I agreed.

The next step was, of course, a cutoff. Welfare finds out that you're in the midst of a college application, already struggling to send one kid to college, having a mid-teen educational running battle with the other kid, and what do they do. Cut off your check, what else?

It goes something like this: "We have received information indicating that your minor child Blahblah is no longer attending school and blah-blahblah, informing you that in order for you to continue to receive your grant this child must attend daily meetings of the Work Help Incentive Program (WHIP) and actively participate in finding employment within three (3) weeks so that we may discontinue your grant and blah-blah."

These "workfare" programs do not find you a job. They do not train you for one. They give you "counselling" and a list of minimum-wage jobs you can apply for. Mainly, you get to sit around in a large plastic waiting room full of screaming brats all day, same scenario as any other welfare-inspired enterprise. If you don't go, they kick your family off welfare. If you do go and don't get a job, your family gets the boot. If you attend and you *do* find work, same thing. The only function I could attribute to this particular program was to get families kicked off welfare. The office was not even accessible to public transportation, except after a long walk through a bad neighborhood.

"I'm not going," said Jessy.

"I guess not," I agreed.

Fortunately, at about this same time, my daughter got bitten by a rat.

The family's assortment of pets included, at this time, several snakes, a tarantula, some chameleons, goldfish, guinea pigs, and two big rats named Jack Mack and Rad Boy. Jessy had let the rats out for exercise one day and for some unknown reason they decided to stage a fight to the death. While she was breaking this up, Jack Mack bit Jessy right through the knuckle of her right hand.

I took her to Childrens' Hospital, where she was admitted for tendon damage and possible infection, the hand wrapped in a huge ball of gauze and suspended from an overhead fixture.

"Very Dr. Seuss," she remarked, flying on drugs, obviously referring to the apparatus.

Thus immobilized, Jessy missed her day at WHIP and I received notice that my welfare grant was to be terminated. However, we could if we wished schedule a "fair hearing," which I requested immediately. It was scheduled to take place in three weeks at Welfare HQ.

Due to fear, I had never requested a "hearing" before. I spent the three weeks quaking with terror. Jessy came with me to the meeting, her long-healed hand heavily bandaged and helplessly suspended in a sling.

The hearings are held in a small plastic office. I had expected a looming courtroom presided over by a Mad Queen.

They provide you with a sort of lawyer, which They call a client advocate, to defend your "rights."

The Defense advocate assigned to me is young, skinny, serious and Jewish. The Prosecutor is old, skinny, severe, and WASPy.

PROSECUTOR: "We have a report from Mrs. So-and-so from the Work Help Incentive Program, which states that your daughter, Jessica, failed to report to her scheduled appointment at the Work Incentive Bureau, and this therefore renders yourself ineligible to receive further aid from the County of Alameda, State of California, United States of America, City of Oakland, for your daughter Jessica Morris, age fifteen, who is judged to be uncooperative with the rules of said County, State, and etc., and is therefore a burden on the System, undeserving of the support of said County and State and Country, and the taxpayers of this Country, and we therefore have terminated your AFDC check, and rightly so."

THE DEFENSE (rummaging through a huge stack of papers—my AFDC file): "Mrs. Ashby, it is your right to present an objection to the County's allegations . . . uh . . . if you have an excuse, let's hear it."

ME (terrified and trembling): "Uh . . . I called Mrs. So-and-so at the WHIP? Excuse me . . . the Work Incentive? Program? Office?" (Involuntarily, I start crying) "And I told her that Jessy couldn't come to the Program that day . . . because she was in the hospital? I did call! I called them!"

THE DEFENSE (rummaging): "Yes, there seems to have been a note made of that." Vibrating with tension or energy or hysteria, maybe all three, she thrusts a barely legible copy of a form on pink onionskin paper at The Prosecutor.

Prosecutor squints at the form, frowning. "Yes, I see. But *this*" (waving the form at The Defense) "Is not *proof* that the Daughter—" Jessy's head snaps up; she looks around at the participants in this farce (The Daughter?? Are they referring to *Me*???) "That The Daughter was actually hospitalized . . . *this*—" (waving form) "only states that a phone call was received by Mrs. So-and-so at the WHIP—excuse me—the Work Help Incentive Program Office on this date. . . ."

I rummage through my own stack of papers and pull out the form I signed when Jessy was released from the hospital. I hand it to The Prosecutor.

PROSECUTOR: "Hmmmm . . ." She focuses an evil eye on Jessy, who has not said a word. Who has been keeping her right arm in the sling, inert, the sling which she hasn't worn since she was discharged from the hospital two weeks before. Who, from time to time, evinces a tiny grimace of pain. Who knows perfectly well that the family can't survive without this AFDC check, negligible as it is, and that without the AFDC coverage she will have no access to medical care, and the rent will not get paid, and bus fare will not be available, and that she is too young to get a legitimate job and too uneducated to get a good job and Mom is already trying to support a houseful of people (including Dudley who has been laid off for a year) who are all liable to wind up homeless in the street. Yet, she feels that she must speak honestly and truthfully.

"Well," Jessy begins, cheerfully, "What happened was that I got in the hospital because I got bit by this rat. I didn't mean to get bit, it just happened. And it hurt a lot, and it swelled up and made me sick. There was this rat, right?"

The Prosecutor and The Defense are both staring at Jessy, as if hypnotized.

JESSY (brightly): "This rat bit me right on the hand. On the right hand, and I'm right-handed, so it was a real bummer. So I couldn't use my hand and it was all red and swollen up. This rat bit me right on the knuckle, and the doctor said that the fluid from the tendon was leaking out, because the rat bit right through the tendon. It was real ugly, and it hurt a lot. The rat didn't mean to do it, but he was fighting with this other rat, and I was trying to stop them from fighting. Right? The other rat's name was Rad Boy. It wasn't his fault, I mean, he didn't start the fight. Who started it was Jack Mack. The rat, I mean. Jack Mack bit me. I knew he didn't really mean to. He was trying to bite Rad Boy. He bit me in the hand, because he thought my hand was Rad Boy, my right hand, right, and they were fighting. I don't know why they were fighting. But they were having this terrible fight, right? And I thought they were really gonna hurt each other. So I'm in the Emergency Room, and this doctor was sticking this needle in my arm. Right in my bloodstream! So I passed out. I just got real dizzy and thirsty, because the doctor was sticking this needle in my bloodstream. But she was a real nice doctor. She said she didn't mean to hurt me, but it was for my own good. So

144

then I woke up, in the Emergency Room, and the doctor asked me What Happened? So I said that a rat bit me. But he didn't mean to. So they put all these blankets on me. And they asked Are You In Pain? And I said What Do You Think??? I got bit by a *rat!* And they said they were gonna put all this medicine in my arm. And I was supposed to go to the WHIP—sorry—the Work Intensive thing? But I was in the hospital with needles...."

"Your AFDC grant will not be discontinued!" states The Prosector, loudly. "This hearing is concluded. You may go now."

JESSY: "So there were all these needles in my arm. And they put this big, *big* bandage on, and they hung my arm from this stick over the bed, up in the air. But then I couldn't *eat,* like, I couldn't hold the fork with my left hand. Because I'm right-handed. Right? And I couldn't call the office with my left hand. I mean, I couldn't do *anything* because I'm right-handed. And my mom came and washed my hair for me. I mean, I couldn't even wash my *hair!!* I really looked *terrible....*"

I take Jessy's elbow and steer her out of the office. As we leave the building, Jessy says "Hey, I did good, huh, Mom."

"You were great," I tell my daughter. "Great!"

Sometimes you can walk on water.

28.
Xmas

I'll never be able to forget the first time I realized that my children were beginning to get excited about Christmas and I had no money. None. We'd only been in Berkeley a few months and I'd been so busy trying to get my AFDC transferred and find a place to live that I hadn't had time to run down any sources for "extras," food giveaways and clothes free-boxes and all this sort of stuff. (Actually, one year, the City of Berkeley sent me a check for $25 with a Christmas card, but that wasn't the year.) I'd bought a twenty-pound bag of rice and ten pounds of onions and a big box of oatmeal, and we were living on that.

I did go to one of the annual toy giveaways. I'd actually received a flyer in the mail — it was widely advertised. This was a national organization devoted to nothing but helping people and scarfing up millions of bucks in donations. So I went down there on the designated day to score some Christmas presents for the kids.

Kids watch TV, and you can't reasonably keep them away from it. When they're very young, they get the message that you get rewarded on the basis of being good or bad, not rich or poor. They learn, but they have to go through a lot first. They don't realize that while the evil slumlord is buying his kids new cars and jet skis for Christmas, with your welfare check, Santa is not writing down the prayers of good little welfare brats on his list.

So I went down to the toy giveaway and stood on line for three hours in the freezing rain with several hundred other welfare moms and grandmoms (and a few dads, to be fair), and finally got to the desk, and gave them my I.D. and proof that I was poor and proof that I really had children, and they wrote in a book as proof that I hadn't stood in the freezing rain for three hours twice, and sent me up to the room where the goodies were.

What they had were the rejects from the Goodwill store. Ragged dolls and dirty stuffed animals, torn scribbled-on books and rusty dented toy trucks and games with half the pieces missing. I couldn't believe it. The other people there couldn't believe it either. (I actually went back the next year because I couldn't believe that the first time had been so disappointing.)

And now, this year, with no children to disappoint, I'm thinking it must be better, because I see Them on TV collecting and giving away new toys to bright-faced happy kids and I know that They couldn't have gotten away with palming off rubbish on us in the name of charity (and scooping up a jillion bucks in donations as they do it) all these years since my children were little.

(I finally solved the Childrens' Miserable Christmas Problem by becoming a master shoplifter of Barbie dolls, G.I. Joes and Tonka Trucks.)

I'm on the bus going downtown when I see (near St. Vinnies's) a miserable little family. A large, sad-faced black woman and four kids sit on a bench holding a collection of ragged dolls, dirty stuffed animals and torn scribbled-on books. Torn Christmas wrapping paper is scattered around their feet. The youngest kid is crying. The older ones have looks that say Oh well, We really didn't expect anything.

And I picture the Generous Givers, waiting until they have ten or twelve Really Good Things, and then calling the media.

They only give away good stuff when the cameras are rolling! What a great, sneaky trick! And They feel no shame in wrapping up an object which belongs in a dumpster, in bright paper and ribbons, and giving it to some poverty-stricken child for Christmas! While the president of the We're-Here-To-Help-You Fund is indicted for placing a quarter of a million bucks in his own pocket and is probably out buying himself a new Mercedes for Christmas!

Journal Entry: I got mad because it was eight-thirty in the evening and They still haven't turned the heat on, and it's Xmas Eve, and just Yuck in general. It's been cold for the past three or four days, about twenty-eight degrees. Puddles outside frozen in the morning. Maybe it'll kill some of the mosquitoes.

D. found a church where we can get a good dinner tomorrow. Otherwise we'd have nothing to eat. Better to starve than go to St. Vinnie's and risk two or three days of cramps and runs.

Journal Entry: We had a great dinner at the church. Lovely food. Thumbtacked around the walls of the dining room were pairs of socks. Socks for the Homeless! They had labels on them. Each pair had a label saying "Gift of Mr and Mrs Whatsis," of "Gift of the So-and-so Church." Thank you Jesus!

Pepsi

Children are almost never seen in the hotel. Once I heard a baby crying on my floor, the fourth floor, for about a week. But I never saw the baby. Perhaps there are kids here, but we don't see or hear them. There is a rule in the Social Services Department that children aren't to live in a place where there are no cooking facilities. A child who lived here would have to do so unknown to Welfare and Children's Services. Can you train a two-year-old to be silent and invisible? People do.

But one day right after Xmas I come downstairs and see a child in the lobby. The child is four or five years old, a little girl, black, wearing dirty little overalls and a happy face T-shirt, baby Reeboks with no socks, and a big green ribbon in her hair. She is sitting on one end of the cardboard couch, alone, staring at the TV. Several of the Doomed, also staring at the tube, seem unaware of her presence.

I go out to get my coffee, read the *Trib* amongst the *Trib* writers, walk over to Sherlock's to look at the books, then walk back to the hotel. The kid is still sitting there staring at the tube.

I go upstairs, take a shower, do some laundry and hang the clothes up in the window to dry, then go down to get my mail. The kid is still there, staring at the TV.

"You letting kids move in here now?" I ask the Desk Guy. He shrugs.

This is extremely dangerous, I think. If I approach the child, someone will think I'm a cop. A welfare cop, or a child molester. A baby-seller or a baby-stealer. A social worker baby-stealer. A welfare cop family breakup artist. Fuck it.

I buy a coke from the coke machine, sit down next to the kid. The kid stares at the tube. The kid is stiff with terror. I should take the hint. Whatever the kid is afraid of is not something to mess with. (It occurs to me later that maybe the kid was afraid of *me*.) The poor little fucker.

"Coke?" I say, offering the Coke to the kid. The kid stares at the tube.

"Would you like a Coke? I got you a Coke," I say.

The kid stares at the tube.

"You speak English?" I ask, emboldened by the fact that nobody has leaped for my throat yet from some hidden recess of the lobby.

The kid gives a tiny little nod, staring at the tube.

Response! I push the can of Coke at the child. "It's for you. You must be thirsty. Coke."

"Pepsi," says the kid, staring at the tube.

"Coke," I repeat, stupidly.

"I don't like Coke. I like Pepsi," says the kid, staring at the. . . .

"But we don't have a Pepsi machine here. We just got a Coke machine."

"Pepsi," says the kid.

"Are you hungry?" I ask. "Want some cheez-its? Food? Where's your mommy?"

The kid stares at the tube. A tear, just one, has left a track down the dirty cheek. "Fuck you," the kid whispers. "Fuck Coke. Pepsi. Pepsi. Go away."

Ashby is struggling up the stairs in the hotel.

She meets an old man who is struggling down the stairs. One of his gnarled old hands is trying to grab onto the wall because the banister rail is loose and shaky. With the other hand, he grips a Bible.

"Store not your treasures upon the earth," intones the old man in a gasping wheeze, "Where moss and dust doth corrupt."

"Moths," says Ashby, pausing to catch her breath on the stairs.

"Moths?" gasps the old man, clutching his Bible closer to his bony chest.

"Moths," says Ashby, regaining her breath and heaving herself up past the old man on the stairs. "Moths and dust doth corrupt. Check it out." She proceeds upward, swinging herself around a corner. The old man is lost to her sight, somewhere below.

"Moths?" She hears the wheezy old voice echoing up the stairwell. "I be damned."

A Temporary 29. Victory

You are not allowed to express your anger. You must bury it, knowing that it is growing cancerous inside you. But how can you express it? After all, what right have *you* to be angry? But you are. Anger grows to be a monster inside you which threatens to go out of control and destroy you. What do you do when this happens? Obviously you can't let the monster gain control.

I usually look for something to do, an outlet, a decompression chamber for the unbearable rage. The rage is a sneaky thing which can be set off by the most commonplace occurrence, dirty dishes in the sink, an overdue library book, an unexpected bill which you don't have the money to pay. And it invariably blows up in your face, eventually, no matter how many sidetracks you find to shuttle it off onto.

Sometimes when I feel a murderous rage start to build up out of control I try to drink myself into unconsciousness. Most of the time, surprisingly, this works. Sometimes it doesn't. As an example, let's put forth the time I threatened to kill Dudley and he called the police. I remember actually begging them to lock me up. If they didn't, I explained, I would kill him. Simple as that.

They made me step out into the street, so that they could bust me for being disorderly in a public place. In a private place, they explained, I'd have to kill him (or do serious damage to his person) before an arrest could legally take place.

I was desperate to go. I felt that I could not tolerate one more moment in his presence, and I really didn't want to commit such a final act as murder. But I was, at the time, capable of it.

At the Oakland jail they took away my shoes and purse and put me in a cell. It was late at night, a Friday night, and the cell was already full. A windowless concrete box about six feet long and four feet wide, with a fifteen-foot-high ceiling. At one end of the box an iron door with a peephole, at the other a toilet/sink combination. Along one side a bench four feet long and one foot wide. A dim bulb enclosed in wire mesh high above. Four or five drunken whores already occupied the cell. They talked among themselves and seemed to know each other, except for a loony Asian woman who kept giggling to herself.

The whores seemed to keep telling me that there would be "trouble" if I didn't stop screaming and banging on the door. I told them to fuck themselves. After a while, I achieved exhaustion and curled up in the tiny space between the toilet and the wall and went to sleep.

As soon as I had retreated into my sought-after blessed unconsciousness, the iron door of the cell banged open and a matron told me to get up and step out of the cell. Cowed and docile and almost asleep, I thought that I was going to be issued a bunk. Everyone else in the cell was still churning around; the middle-aged Asian woman had been giggling insanely for hours.

The matron marched me down the hall and put me in a box the same size as the other one, by myself. This box had no bench, no fixtures of any kind except a hole in one corner of the floor. The light bulb high overhead seemed unbearably bright. I was left alone with the monster.

Something in me recognizes unnecessary torture. I screamed, kicked, banged my head on the iron door until I saw stars. I had forgotten that you really do see stars. I chewed the insides of my wrists to open the veins, determined to kill myself. It didn't work. Finally, battered and bruised to utter exhaustion by my own personal monster, I went to sleep.

I awakened later feeling like I'd been run over by a truck. I knew I had temporarily conquered the monster, but I'd kicked my own ass pretty thoroughly in the process. I was a beaten animal, scarcely human.

I slumped against the peephole and when a matron passed by I croaked for water. I had never been so thirsty and I wanted a bit of water more than anything I've ever wanted in life. She said no, I couldn't have any, because she "didn't like my attitude." The next time she walked by I asked for the time. No.

So I didn't know if it was night or day, or how long I'd been there, or would be there, without access to a drink of water or anything else. From the cell next to mine came outbursts of screaming; what sounded like a young girl screaming in uncontrollable terror and bewilderment, shrieking for her mama.

"Mama!! Mama!! I want my Mama! Mama Pleeeease come get me!! Pleeease!"

She'd been screaming for hours.

When I was finally released from the cell I was taken to a little room with a metal desk and chairs. I was searched in a superficial way, asked to turn my pockets and socks inside out. I wondered why this hadn't been done the night before; I could have been loaded with hidden knives, drugs, razor blades, poison. The matrons on the morning shift were cool and professional, almost sympathetic. They produced my bag from somewhere and went through the contents with professional thoroughness. They found one loose pill, a Tagamet, for ulcers. "We could charge you with this," they said. "I have a prescription," I told them. "It has to be in a bottle with the proper label," they informed me.

But they didn't charge me. They let me keep my asthma inhaler, which was properly labeled. They told me I'd go to court that day.

They let me make my phone call. Dudley was annoyed when I

asked for fifty bucks for bail. He hung up. Click.

They fingerprinted me and took my picture. When They told me to wash the fingerprint ink off my hands, I finally got a drink of water. My mouth was so dry and coated that it didn't recognize the wetness. They sent me to the nurse, who bandaged my wrists and gave me two aspirin.

I was put in a dormitory which held about twenty double-decker bunks, and given a sheet, a blanket, and a towel. A list of names was called for morning court and mine wasn't on it. I was too sick to care.

They called me for afternoon court, along with fifteen or twenty other female prisoners. One girl in the dorm had possession of an illicit comb. It was greasy and filthy. We all used it. They gave us back our shoes. We spent the afternoon in several different "holding cells" in the courthouse. At six or seven P.M. we were taken back to the dorm.

There is a TV attached high on the wall in one corner of the dorm. The matron can change the channel from her office. There is a buzzer in the dorm to summon the matron in an emergency. Usually they don't answer. There is a metal table with benches bolted to the floor by the door, where meals are served. There is not room for everyone at the table.

Aside from myself, another drunk, and a traffic violator (her car registration had expired), all the women in the dorm are whore/addicts. Most of these have been busted on the job, wearing short-shorts, halter tops and wigs. In the dorm, which is air-conditioned to the max, they wrap themselves in their sheets to keep warm. They are generally allowed to don their wigs for court: some of the resulting transformations are astonishing.

My dorm-mates don't seem to mind being in jail. A familiar place, and most of them know each other from previous incarcerations or from the street. They talk endlessly about tricks, dope, favorite motels, other busts, the cops they like and the cops they hate, pimps, boyfriends and husbands, TV shows. They watch the soap operas faithfully and lament over the problems of *All My Children*. They discuss the ups and downs of their profession with professional pride.

"Why should I break my ass at McDonalds for three bucks an hour? I can make $500 in one night on the street," boasts a gorgeous little black teenager wearing a leotard under her sheet.

"I'll *never* stop 'ho-in and shootin' smack," declares an older whore with a practically toothless grin.

"Well, *I* ain't a 'ho, I a *thief*," claims another, bewigged and hot-pantsed. She entertains us with stories about the dumb johns she's robbed.

They talk about the county jail, Santa Rita, longing for its relative comforts. "I can't *wait* to get on that Santa Rita bus," is a constant refrain.

The next morning we are called for court again, issued our shoes (and wigs), and taken back through the long subterranean maze to the courthouse. The elevators have built-in cages to prevent hijacking.

There are only a few women in the holding cell with me this time, two white whores and two black whores. One of the white whores has been brought from the jail ward at Highland Hospital, her hands swollen like horrible red balloons with cellulitis from shooting dope. Her arms and legs are covered with abscess scars. "I guess I must be the abscessinist 'ho you ever did see," she explains cheerfully. She tells us that her husband is on Death Row for armed robbery and murder.

There is also a gaunt, middle-aged black woman, wearing a buttoned-up trench coat, who never speaks. This woman radiates such hostility and hatred that every hair on her head stands straight out, vibrating, and her eyes burn like laser beams.

It is cold in the holding tank, colder even than our cells. The scantily-dressed whores huddle together at one end, shivering. Some time around noon we are given stale baloney sandwiches and a half-pint of orange Kool-Aid.

At three P.M. we are down to our last shared cigarette, but we have no more matches. The furious black woman still has cigarettes and matches. Being closest to her on the bench, I politely ask her for a light. She ignores me, vibrating, laser eyes aimed straight ahead at the wall.

"Maybe she don't like Whitey," one of the white whores suggests.

One of the black whores then gets up to approach the woman and is also ignored. She goes back to the huddle. After a few minutes of whispering, both of the whores, white and black, get up to make a last desperate appeal. They beg in unison. "We don't even want a *match*, lady, just a light off your cigarette. . . ."

This time they are met with such a horrendous torrent of abuse that they back away in startled alarm. No fun to be locked up with a maniac and no one can hear you scream. The angry woman remains rigid, electrified, staring at the opposite wall, calling us every kind of a motherfucker and screaming at us to "get outa my *face!*"

Then she proceeds to smoke one cigarette after another, carefully extinguishing each match and grinding each butt on the gritty floor until no spark remains.

At five o'clock, when all the judges have gone home or to the nearest bar, we are put in a larger holding tank which smells of men: smoke and sweat and fear. We are then told that the women don't get to go to court until all the men have been to court.

At seven P.M. we are finally released to an empty courtroom, where we sign release forms for a bailiff, a young guy in a uniform who addresses each one of us personally, kindly, and jokes with us in a good-natured way. "And take better care of yourself," he tells me, looking up from my bandaged wrists, into my eyes. A jolt. My clobbered senses are beginning to reawaken, and I feel a twinge of astonishment—he seems to really care.

I go out to the street. Nothing has changed, but nothing looks familiar. Not better, just different. I wander around for twenty minutes, looking for the jail building where I can reclaim my possessions. I call Dudley, who finally agrees to come pick me up at the jail.

When I see him coming down the street, I start to get angry all over again.

30.
The Cave

There was the time when I was so angry that I ran a quarter of a mile through the storm drain and jumped into a pool of quicksand. I hadn't known it was quicksand—it just looked like a knee-deep, rather stagnant pond to me. It was well below street level, and I don't suppose anyone would have heard me scream if I'd chosen to, but I didn't. I was in one of those states where rage completely overpowers fear. I just said "Oh, well," as I sank. The quicksand was only knee-deep. I climbed out, soaked to the hips in rather slimy water, and made my way back through the tunnel feeling more foolish by the minute as my anger drained away.

I am normally a fairly patient and good-natured person, and few things can engender a murderous (or self-destructive) rage in me. A housing crisis is one of them. Having been through so many of them, and having been forced to move so many times (a hundred?) mainly for financial reasons, one would think that I would have become used to it and could take it in stride, not let it upset me so, but it seems that the opposite is true. Every time I have to face the ordeal of moving, the anger increases exponentially, until now even a voluntary move will

157

render me temporarily insane and physically incapacitated.

When I underwent the Experience of the Quicksand, I was getting ready to lose my student apartment on campus. I had no money to rent another apartment, of course, and had Jessy living with me. Through the conniving of the student apartment complex manager, my security deposit wasn't returned (she made enough loot by not returning students' deposits to buy a new car), and I applied to the school for a small grant. This was my last resort, and I thought they *should* help me after scarfing up fifty thousand dollars in student loans and grants through me. The sum I asked for was nothing. They'd spend that much painting the flagpole or planting a few petunias.

Then the English Department, seeing my growing despair (me being *their* creature, after all), gave me a grant sufficient to rent The Bunker. The Administration promptly refused to issue the check.

"Why? Why? Why? Why?" I begged.

"Because if you hadn't been a student at this school, you wouldn't have gotten the grant, therefore we have the right to take it away," was Their line of reasoning.

Being Them, they were able to say this in such a way that it seemed to make sense.

So it all looked hopeless. I'll be homeless in the street.

I'll jump.

But do you really, really want to jump?

I'll jump anyway.

What about Jessy?

I'll just stay here then, until They figure out some way to get rid of me.

But They'd torture you.

In slow, exquisite, final ways. They'd make you feel like pond scum at the bottom of a well. You have a spirit left? They'll trash whatever's left of it. They know how to do these things; They've had lots of practice.

And besides, I really hate this place.

It's only bearable if you can go somewhere else once in a while.

A sorry rat only has one hole.

I've been in this one much too long.

You don't know what it's like to really hate a place, or person or thing, until you've sat through some sad, stupid scenario a hundred times, a thousand times, due to simple immobility. Is it a contradiction that the homeless and near-homeless seem to be the most immobile segment of the population?

The rich, after all, are always moving around. The town house, the summer house, the boat, the villa, the islands, the club, the camp. They're staying at the most luxurious place you can imagine and they're sick of it in two weeks. "So we flew down to Cadoga for the film festival."

They know how important it is not to get stuck.

They probably don't know what it's like to have absolutely no place to go.

So I'll get even with Them. I'll go live in the storm drain and sneak out at night and raid and loot. (Jessy can surely find some friend to stay with.) I'll institute a reign of terror on the campus! The security guards all know me—I used to work for Security. They'll think I'm still a student! They'll never know that I'm the one, their Midnight Marauder, pillaging and plundering at will. The graduate student from hell!

(Shudder.)

The Caves

There are caves out by the Cliff House in San Francisco; some made by the sea and some by people, and there are artificial boulders, hollow, large enough to crawl inside, and there is even a phony cliff, which looks real from any distance, with little stairways built into it that you can't see unless you know right where they are.

There are caves in the Oakland hills, in the Berkeley hills; there are mine shafts and the caldera of dead volcanoes. There are storm drains and places where creeks and streams have been diverted underground; you can walk beneath the streets and crawl far under the freeways. You can step right off the edge of civilization.

Take a flashlight, a can of spray paint, and a soul that is free of guilt. The reason for bringing a flashlight should be obvious. The spray paint is so you can leave your mark in the Beyond, and the guilt-free soul is for when you are deep in some tunnel in the earth where there is no light and no sound and you find yourself being assaulted by panic and stripped naked in front of your gods—whoever or whatever they may be.

There is an opening in the rock by the Cliff House in San Francisco, obviously man-made, just large enough for one or two people to enter walking upright. It is floored with sand and slants down, turning, so that when one is four or five yards inside one is in total darkness. Somewhere beneath or near this man-made tunnel is a sea cave, carved into the rock by the crashing waves over millennia, and in the depths of the tunnel one can hear and actually feel the waves crashing in, the vibrations of millions of tons of water hurtling against millions of tons of rock, and one suddenly realizes that it never stops—it never ever stops.

Ignoring the smell of the millions of urinations which have taken place, somewhat sacrilegiously you may think, along the walls of this cavity, you grope along with your penlight, and finally come to the end of the tunnel. The tunnel ends like this: a widening, a little room floored with sand, and on the opposite wall, the dead-end wall, is embedded a large, rusty iron ring. And you might think "What the hell?" but you don't have time to think further because the waves are crashing in. And the rock is vibrating with each crash. And each crash gurgles and roars around you as though you were inside an enormous toilet which is at this minute being flushed. And you expect to be flushed away, realizing that you are just another turd as far as the almighty sea is concerned. And as soon as you realize this, you are elevated to the gods for judgement, and so you flee up the shaft to the sunny surface. And a long time later you remember that iron ring embedded in the wall at the bottom of the cave and you wonder what, or who, was originally meant to be chained to it. . . .

(Shudder.)

· · ·

Well, maybe I won't go live in the storm drain. I'll crash on Adeline's couch until we work something out. That's the civilized way, the college-educated way.

But then a favorite teacher/mentor comes to my rescue, and hands me a check to pay the first-last-security on The Bunker.

"I don't know if I can pay you back." I tell her.

"Some day you'll be rich," she says.

I like to think that of course this is the kind of thing I'd do, if. So I can accept calmly and gracefully. It's more money than I've ever had at one time in my life.

Live in a *cave? Me??* I wouldn't last a day. Besides, I'd need my books and my typewriter, and where could I plug it in? And a lamp. And lots of food and drink. A hot tub and jacuzzi. TV and a VCR, at least one. Quadrophonic sound. Computers to run everything. A Mercedes. A private jet. . . .

The Bunker was tiny, but it would do. I could pay the rent as long as Jessy kept her job. I had room for my books and my paintings and my typewriter. I needed nothing else. I would do nothing but write. I would write my way out.

Writer At Work

My Garden

WRITER AT WORK: (types) "My Garden."

INTERRUPTER (from here on to be known as IT) gets up from seat in corner where IT has been quietly reading/watching TV/ listening to music/whatever, and walks up behind writer's (to be identified as WRT) chair to read over WRT's shoulder whatever it is that WRT is writing.

IT (reading): "My Garden."

WRT (sighs): "I'm trying to write something about my garden."

IT: "Well, don't let *me* interrupt you!"

WRT: (types) "Once I had a beautiful garden. . . ."

IT: "Do you mean in a figurative sense?"

WRT: (types) "I loved my garden." Says: "What?"

IT: "I mean, was it a literal garden?"

WRT: (types) "I spent a month turning over the soil." Says: "A literary garden?"

IT: "I mean, was it a real garden, in the literal sense?"

WRT: (types) "With a shovel. I only had time to dig down eight or ten inches."

IT: "Or a garden in the intellectual or spiritual sense?"

WRT: (types) "So I couldn't plant anything like carrots or potatoes, or anything that needed deep roots."

IT: "You know, a Garden of the Psyche, so to speak. . . ."

WRT: (types) "Because I had to wait for the soil to dry out a bit, because there's no point in digging in mud."

IT: "A Garden of the Mind."

WRT: (types) "But to turn over the earth before it was completely dry and hard, which would have been too difficult to do with just a shovel." Says: "What?"

IT: "Of ideas. A place for ideas to blossom and grow. . . ."

WRT: (types) "Because it needs to absorb oxygen."

IT: "To bear fruit, fruit of the mind."

WRT: (types) "Because if it's too wet it's mud and no point. If it's too dry you get cement, cement, seeds can't—you can't grow seeds under cement." Says: "What?"

IT: "A figurative garden, you know, a Garden of the Mind."

WRT: "I heard you, you don't have to scream. No. It was a real garden. I was growing this garden back behind this place I used to live at on Blah-blah Street. . . ."

IT: "Well, you don't have to get an *attitude* about it!"

WRT (patiently): "I was just trying to write this stupid little thing about my garden."

IT: "Well, *sorry* I ruined it!"

WRT: "Hey, you're not *good* enough to ruin anything I write." (types): "Zucchini grows really well in this climate, but zucchini is a cheap shot, so I didn't plant any. Instead, I planted pumpkins."

IT: "I was just trying to be helpful. Sniff."

WRT: (types) "Just for the hell of it. The vine grew all over the fence, so it wasn't in the way. I got four pumpkins, but two rotted on the vine. But on Halloween, I had one pumpkin for each child. They went out in the garden and picked their own pumpkins on Halloween. It was great."
IT (still looking over WRT's shoulder): "That's *so* corny!"
WRT: (types) "I grew two rows of corn, too. It didn't get much more than five feet high, but there were four or five ears on each stalk."
IT: "I'll just *leave*, then, if I'm in your way."
WRT: (types) "The ears were small, not more than eight or ten inches long. And funny-looking. But we ate them anyway. They were better than anything from the supermarket." Says: "What?"
IT: "I didn't mean to *bother* you."
WRT: (types) "We grew some lettuce. Earwigs lived in the lettuce leaves. We fed the earwigs to our Venus Fly Trap."

31.

Looking

Journal Entry: I got my Section 8 certificate yesterday. I had received a notice in the mail to attend a briefing at the housing authority office in Rodeo, took BART to the end of the line and found two busses to Rodeo, got on the wrong one, and after an hour or so this bus left me off at the wrong end of town.

Had to walk all the way across town, but I'd left three hours before the appointment to leave time for fuckups, because I'd already missed my first appointment, weeks ago, the notice about the scheduled briefing having arrived after the briefing had taken place. Not my fault, but They only let you have so much leeway.

The certificate wasn't what I'd expected ("Take these forms to Window B and they'll issue you an apartment") — It seems that I must find my own place and it must meet all these govt. standards like running water and electricity and a toilet that works, then I have to negotiate a contract with the landlord and the housing authority, and then I'm stuck with whatever I can work out for one year or I break the contract and lose my certificate.

All these responsibilities I'm supposed to be mature and adult about. Without fucking up. Can I do this? Can I handle all this in a mature adult fashion?

I have eight weeks to find an apartment and I want to live in Berkeley. My second choice is San Francisco, but I don't have the resources to apartment-search there.

In Berkeley, most apartment listings are with private agencies. I've tried them several times in the past, never found anything suitable through them, and wound up losing my payment. The cost used to be about forty dollars—I'm afraid to ask what it is now, and anyway I don't have it, and I suspect these services don't even list Section 8 units.

I refuse to even look in Oakland. The papers are full of Section 8 vacancies and they even use come-ons. "One month rent free!" "Redwood hot tub!" "Se habla Español!" I've seen enough of Oakland. When Jessy and I were apartment-searching for The Bunker, we saw stuff which is better left undescribed. I'm fed up with uncleanable bathrooms, insane landlords, crack houses, automatic weapons, bars on every window, teenage gangs at the bus stop. I especially don't want to deal with the Oakland Housing Authority, who will only talk to you through the glass in a bullet-proof booth.

"Who are you to be picky?" asks that little sandpaper voice in my head.

I don't know. I don't know who I am to be picky. Maybe I don't know who I am at all. But I'm going to have my own place and it's not going to be another trash heap if I can help it.

Journal Entry: Woke at two A.M. with residual pain from yesterday's food poisoning. Horrible stabbing pains in the gut. I'll survive.

Went to scheduled reevaluation interview for SSI today. My legs felt like wet noodles and my hair dripped with sweat. Astonishingly sharp pains at random intervals; my digestive system felt ripped to shreds.

The interviewer, a young woman, asked me if I was OK, with genuine concern. I must have looked really bad. I kept my sense of humor.

When she asked if I required help to bathe, dress, and feed myself, I said "Not yet."

I went to the Berkeley Housing Authority and found that they publish a list of available Section 8 apartments every week. Most of them are in an area which I call Crack City. I lived in this area once and it was awful then, and this was long before They invented crack. I called several numbers in areas that looked better and got answering machines. "Please leave your number. . . ."

I applied to the SSI office for moving money and to Alameda County for a security deposit check which will be made out to my prospective landlord when I find one.

Journal Entry: So far, every call I've made about an apartment has been answered by a machine: ". . . We'll call you back." And of course I have no phone, no phone jack in the room even, and I've been leaving Jessy's number, but then if and when they call back they'll get *her* machine, so I'm trying to figure out what to do. There has to be a way.

Journal Entry: Jessy's number is not working for me. Next week when I go to the BHA for the new list I'll ask them if they have any suggestions.

Journal Entry: I went to the Berkeley Housing Authority yesterday and explained my problem with the phone calls. They were taken aback. They told me my problem was unique and they couldn't think of any suggestions to offer about how to solve it.

A lot of the people I've called who don't use answering machines, who actually answer the telephone, seem to be straight-off-the-boat or out-of-the-woodwork types who don't seem to speak English too well.

I achieved contact with the Suspicious Hispanic: "*Wha* joo wan??"; the Brutal Greco/Roman "Yah. Yah. I tellim, yah,"; the Asio/Indian Tycoon "You got certificate? You *sure* you got? You *bring* it!" And of course the inevitable Old Redneck Couple "Wal, you'll have ta talk ta the Missus . . ." who want to know what *church* I belong to, and they're all impossible, impossible, none of them would ever leave me alone for a minute—"You do *what?* You write *what?*"

I also discover that the apartments on Housing Authority lists have not necessarily been inspected yet, or *ever.* I find myself running around, peering into the weirdest places: damp basements, dusty attics, windowless, converted garages and chicken-coops. A tiny shack-out-back, for instance, listed as a one-bedroom unit, turned out to have no living room. Just a tiny kitchen, closet-sized bath, and microscopic bedroom (it *did* have a bedroom at least) that some pitiful old couple was counting on renting out for upwards of six hundred bucks a month.

This goes on for several weeks. I have a phone booth in the BART station as my headquarters, a secret stash of quarters, and a will not to fail. But I'm thinking: What if it's really impossible? What if it's just another trick and you have to pay somebody off, but they won't tell you who or even that you have to do it, and if you ask they'll nail you. If you have to ask, you're obviously too stupid to live.

Journal Entry: I finally made contact with a landlord phone-to-phone, went to his office for actual person-to-person communication, and I think, I hope, I pray, that I have an apartment.

The guy wanted the BHA forms; BHA wouldn't give them to me and ordered me to go to Contra Costa to get original forms/records/affidavits/proofs/verifications. I went. Five-hour round-trip on BART/bus/foot. The Contra Costa Housing Authority gave me the stuff in a *sealed envelope* and ordered me not to peek. So much for taking mature adult responsibility for self.

The Sealed Envelope was then delivered by mature adult self back to BHA in a civilized manner (I didn't peek!), although I thought about walking into the place with the Sealed Envelope pinned to my chest along with a note from my mom.

One of the forms was a checklist which I was supposed to have filled out (without peeking). I was supposed to have gone through the prospective unit and checked "satisfactory" or "unsatisfactory" in little boxes describing aspects of the unit (windows/doors/lights/etc.) The Housing Authority gave me the list, which I then took to the office of the landlord, who snatched it out of my hand and checked "satisfactory" on everything, handed it back—here you go, mature responsible adult— I'm not gonna say anything or protest, right? *I just wanna get off the street!* HUD help me!

Anyway, HUD willing, I should have my own apartment in two weeks.

Journal Entry: I checked with BHA yesterday, and have to call back today to find out when they're going to inspect my apartment. It has to be inspected before the rental agreement can be signed. My check is already almost gone; I had to pay rent for the hotel room, another month's rent on my storage locker, rent for my post office box, and I loaned Jessy some loot to pay *her* rent, and that's the way it goes. I sent in my forms for moving money (not that I have much to move) to SSI. Hope I checked all the little boxes right.

Journal Entry: Went to Hayward, to the main office of Alameda County Social Services, to get my check for security deposit and last month's rent on my new apartment. I talked to some woman on the house phone in the waiting room.

The place was almost empty. A white woman with a battered face and two fresh black eyes was talking to a young yuppie social worker, crying and desperate.

The woman I talked to on the house phone said, Didn't I know tomorrow was Christmas Eve? And everybody was going on Christmas Vacation? What kind of person *was* I, to give these people a hard time when they were getting ready for Christmas? I would just have to wait until the Christmas vacation was over, after New Year's, when everybody was back at work.

But I have to pay this *now!* I have to get this apartment *now*, before somebody else takes it! Fuck your Christmas vacation! Surely you have time to fill out *one more form!*

I hung up the phone and sat down on a bench in the waiting room, crying. I will not leave this office until you help me. I will not. I will fucking *die* right here in your fucking waiting room . . . and Merry Christmas, you bastards.

I sat there crying for half an hour, and finally a woman came down to talk to me. She was kind and concerned. She said she was sorry . . . she hadn't realized that I was in such bad shape. She would authorize my check right away, and I could pick it up tomorrow. Yes, I *would* be able to get my apartment. After all, it's Christmas!!!

And so it came to pass. . . .

Peace on Earth and goodwill to all you fuckers!

On the way home on BART, I find myself listening to a teenager who is explaining his method for dealing with homelessness to a group of Asian college students across the aisle. This kid is neatly dressed, his clothes clean though a bit frayed, his hair short and carefully combed. He holds a pillowcase full of laundry on his lap.

He has a storage locker, he says, and every week or so he collects his dirty laundry from the locker and goes to the Homeless Resources Center where he takes a shower and puts on clean clothes and does his laundry in their machine.

He sometimes sleeps on BART or at the airport. As long as you don't show up in the same place too often. Sometimes a group of kids will get together and get a room somewhere, but he'd rather keep to himself.

"I'd rather go it alone," he says. The Asian students are nodding and smiling. The train is pulling into a station.

He looks at me, sees that I am listening to his spiel. His expression changes suddenly. "They drive you crazy," he says. "They make you crazy, and then They get rid of you. They have to figure out how to get rid of you."

He gets up and walks quickly from the train, holding his laundry bag.

32. A Sorry Rat

The Big City Cat

There was a cat who lived on our block in New York City, West 98th Street.

The cat lived behind a vacant building on the corner of Amsterdam and 98th, the stinking, garbagey rubble of what had been an Irish bar. You'd be walking past the entrance to the alley behind the ex-building, and this cat would be there. Sometimes it would say something in a little squeaky rasp, and you'd look over to the alley entrance, and this cat would be sitting there. It was a hideous wreck of a cat, a crooked skeleton covered with mangy flea-ridden fur. But if you stopped there, it would talk to you. It would say "Spare change?"

Or whatever the cat equivalent of "Spare change" is. And you'd ask yourself if you might have something in your backpack or your purse—popcorn, a cracker, anything. And if you didn't, the cat would still come out to be petted, and would settle for a bit of attention.

After a while, you'd start to hear about the cat from other people. Family, friends, neighbors. People would slip a bit of food into their pocket as they were leaving. "For the cat, you know, the cat. . . ."

So we started talking about the cat from time to time.

"This cat loves people."

"After the way it's been abused!"

"If there was an Auschwitz for cats, this one would be from there."

"It's an abandoned cat. It belonged to somebody once."

"Somebody loved it once."

"But usually when cats are abandoned they get feral and won't come near you, and hate the world."

"Well, *this* cat doesn't hate the world."

"Maybe it's a mentally retarded cat and doesn't have enough sense to hate the world."

"Maybe it's lost its instincts."

"But it loves people! It loves *us*! It *talks* to us. Even if you don't have anything to feed the cat, it loves you anyway."

"What a strange cat."

"The cat is fucked up."

"There's something horribly wrong with this cat."

"Maybe it's a communist cat, part of a communist plot."

"*Everyone* is feeding the cat now."

"But it doesn't get any fatter."

"And it won't fight. It has no scars. It's a pacifist cat."

"The cat is fucked up."

"It's a hopeless cat."

"Fucked up."

So this rich guy on the block went and got the cat and took it to the vet, and got its worms cleaned out, and the mange and fleas and lice and everything. And it lives in a huge, wealthy apartment, and eats smoked salmon and caviar. And the rich guy says that the cat is the most wonderful and astounding creature he's ever known. And the cat is now his pride and joy.

. . .

Moving In

I retrieve my stuff from my storage locker, a futon and bedding, dishes and pots, my typewriter and desk, my old manuscripts and paintings, and about five thousand books. Boxes of my Stuff, miscellaneous Stuff.

I have my own little apartment now, with all my Stuff around me, so I should be deliriously happy. Instead, I find that I have become so paranoid that I can barely leave the place. For years.

For the first six months I basically just sit there waiting for the Knock On The Door. It will be the Landlord, the Housing Authority, HUD, the cops or the FBI.

"We made a mistake. You can't have an apartment after all. Where did you ever get the idea that we'd let you have your own *apartment?*"

If I leave the place long enough to go to the corner store, I'll come back and find the locks changed and a note nailed to the doorpost "We made a mistake. . . ."

Journal Entry: I didn't go out today. When I go out in the street I become terrified. I feel like prey. California is such a predatory place, after all. It's even worse than New York, because there at least it's blatant and obvious. Predators look like what they are. Here, it's all covered up and disguised to look like something else. You can only tell by the eyes, when you can see them.

They're all actors here. You feel that you have to make eye-contact, and sometimes that alone is enough to do you in.

One day about two weeks after I move in there is a Knock On The Door. It's Dudley, with his stuff. Can he stay a few days until he finds a new place? He tells a long story about how he owes rent and Patels are trying to steal his unemployment check, and blahblahblah.

"Sure, come on in." He can go to the corner store for me.

(This is one of the major fears when you finally get an apartment in a place where you once lived in the street: that some old street buddy will find out where you live. "Hey! I haven't seen you in years! Where are you living? You living around here? Wait a minute while I get my stuff. . . ."

And you have to let them in. Because you've had such good luck and you might spoil it if you don't give *them* a chance, but what happens is that instead of you rescuing them from the Street *they* end up dragging *you* back into the gutter with them.)

After about six months of this I decide it's time to start writing again. At least I can do *that*. I get the ancient Selectric tuned up, score a ream of paper, and start keeping a journal again. My first typed journal. What I want to do is not only record the events of my more or less eventless life, but to try to figure out what happened to me—what led me to my current state. Maybe by doing this I can find a way to recover, to be communicative, productive, to join "society."

Writing

It's a good place, an easy place to begin. The banal present and the remote past, two planets farthest from the sun of my personal madness. I'm circling myself like the sick wolf circling the starving prospector on the frozen tundra of Alaska. It's probably dangerous, but there's nothing else to do now.

I wake up every morning in an avalanche of pain and rage and fear, wishing I didn't have to wake up, understanding now why Adeline's first waking thought would be Need A Drink and why this will be provided, only this and nothing else.

How much influence does the past have on us? Not even my own personal past, with which I am dreading the inevitable confrontation, but the thoughts and feelings and actions which took place on distant links of the chain back to oblivion. Are they still taking place in me? Are the Nomad and the Settler battling to the death over the barren stretch of wilderness inside my head? Do you get to have some peace after they've killed each other?

Maybe I should just spend the rest of my life reading, in total escape. I can start by rereading the five thousand books I already have. I'll turn to the wall and never write another word. I should probably be struck blind for saying that; blindness would be a fitting punishment for me.

But I don't feel exactly as if I need to be punished, as though I were still an ignorant child. Actually, I was never an ignorant child. Dumb and stupid, maybe, but not ignorant. I never ignored anything. It can be a problem, being unable to ignore. I could watch TV, listen to the radio, and read a book at the same time, while eating, and still not be able to ignore what was being discussed (or argued about) in my supposedly ignorant presence. Did this hypersensitivity fragment my senses, and are the voices that I should have been able (or should have had the sense to) ignore still rocketing around in my skull? If I can remember those old radio programs. . . .

I should build a freeway of the mind, in order not to be distracted by every little side street. I should be in the middle of the Greenland ice cap.

I sit at the old typewriter, which is a distraction in itself (is it breaking down again?), and wonder where the next interruption will come from. If it's a person, I promise myself I won't let my anger run away with me this time. The anger is so pointless and stupid (How could they know, for god's sake, that I was trying to type?) that I can't believe it's even *me*.

At night, deep in the night, I lie on my torture rack while the rat runs on its wheel in my head. I try to think about good things.

There are no good things.

Of course there are, *you* just don't want to think about them.

But the rat likes its wheel.

You enjoy the torture.

You feed on it. It feeds you.

I analyze my nightmares.

I can't tell dreams from reality any more, because it's *all* bad.

The sorry rat.

Dreams are a metaphor for whatever you try to ignore.

Journal entry: Berkeley. Today was the Fourth of July. I talked to a real Indian this morning—a pathetic, beaten-up character named John Red Deer who was sitting in the street crying. A real bad Injun.

I was washing my clothes at the laundromat on Shattuck and went out to talk to a fat little Mexican guy who was putting quarters in the parking meter. He was doing his laundry, too. I told him he didn't have to feed the meter because it was a holiday, the Fourth of July.

After we'd talked for a few minutes he went back inside and I started talking to this miserable Injun who was sitting on the sidewalk next to the laundromat. A perfect Hollywood Injun with long black braids.

I asked him if he wanted a cigarette. He didn't want one of his own, but a puff of the one I was smoking. OK. He wanted to communicate something to me. He had something to tell me, but I had nothing to tell him.

He said that he was in touch with the spirits, and could call down an eagle from the sky. I told him that calling an eagle down wouldn't work here, but if he could call down *money* from the sky he might be able to get by.

He said he was a Sioux, from South Dakota or somewhere, and had been here a few weeks. He started crying again, and said that this place was *horrible*; he couldn't fucking *believe* this place! I suggested that he should probably go back to South Dakota or wherever.

Then he told me that he could call down the spirits, that he could call down the spirit of my mother. I told him my mom wasn't dead. He said he'd call anyway, and would I like to talk to my mom's spirit? I said no, the last thing I wanted to do today was talk to my mom. So he asks me for a kiss, and then tries to tear my clothes off in the street. I retreat to the rear of the laundromat and start yanking my not-quite-dry clothes out of the dryer.

From now on I *will* remember to keep my mouth shut if it's the last thing I do.

I used to do a lot of writing in laundromats. White noise.